THE
AUEN
FOUNDATION

The purchase of this book
was made possible
by a generous grant from
The Auen Foundation.

THE HIGHWAYMAN

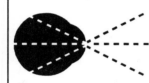

This Large Print Book carries the
Seal of Approval of N.A.V.H.

THE HIGHWAYMAN

CRAIG JOHNSON

THORNDIKE PRESS
A part of Gale, Cengage Learning

GALE
CENGAGE Learning·

Farmington Hills, Mich • San Francisco • New York • Waterville, Maine
Meriden, Conn • Mason, Ohio • Chicago

GALE
CENGAGE Learning®

Copyright © 2016 by Craig Johnson.
A Walt Longmire Mystery.
Thorndike Press, a part of Gale, Cengage Learning.

Thorndike Press® Large Print Mystery.
The text of this Large Print edition is unabridged.
Other aspects of the book may vary from the original edition.
Set in 16 pt. Plantin.

LIBRARY OF CONGRESS CATALOGING-IN-PUBLICATION DATA

Names: Johnson, Craig, 1961- author.
Title: The highwayman / Craig Johnson.
Description: Large print edition. | Waterville, Maine : Thorndike Press, 2016. | © 2016 | Series: A Walt Longmire mystery | Series: Thorndike Press large print mystery
Identifiers: LCCN 2016014308 | ISBN 9781410489081 (hardback) | ISBN 1410489086 (hardcover)
Subjects: LCSH: Longmire, Walt (Fictitious character)—Fiction. | Sheriffs—Fiction. | Wyoming—Fiction. | BISAC: FICTION / Mystery & Detective / General. | GSAFD: Mystery fiction.
Classification: LCC PS3610.O325 H54 2016 | DDC 813/.6—dc23
LC record available at http://lccn.loc.gov/2016014308

Published in 2016 by arrangement with Viking, an imprint of Penguin Publishing Group, a division of Penguin Random House LLC

Printed in the United States of America
1 2 3 4 5 6 7 20 19 18 17 16

*For the Wyoming Highway Patrol,
the true highwaymen and women.*

And still of a winter's night, they say, when the wind is in the trees, when the moon is a ghostly galleon tossed upon cloudy seas, when the road is a ribbon of moon-light over the purple moor, a highwayman comes riding.

— Alfred Noyes, "The Highwayman"

ACKNOWLEDGMENTS

One evening when we were driving through the tunnels of the Wind River Canyon Scenic Byway, my wife and I came upon a stranded motorist frantically grinding his starter in an attempt to get his car going. He was an older gentleman and it's a pretty hazardous place to be sitting if traffic were to come along, so I told Judy to go up to the north end and flag any cars that might be heading southbound.

Making sure he had the car in neutral and his foot off the brake, I began pushing the stalled-out car the fifty yards to the turnout between the tunnels, all the while hoping that some unknowing motorist wouldn't come whistling into the darkness and slam into the both of us.

I think those minutes with my back against the sedan might've been the longest in my life, but once I got him out and safely parked he was able to use his cell phone and call for help. I ran through the tunnel to let Judy know what was going on and then returned to sit with him until the tow truck arrived. When I walked back through the gloom, my imagination started to work . . .

I'll be honest — like most I love a good ghost story and every time I've driven through the Wind River Canyon I've felt as if there was one there just waiting to be put down on paper.

My humble contribution to the genre wouldn't have been possible without the influence of Charles Dickens's "The Signal-Man," which I consider to be one of the world's finest written ghost stories. After rereading it, I began thinking about how I could update it in the face of a modern age with so much technology. I remember talking to my good friend Jim Thomas about the Wind River Canyon, one of numerous magical places in the wonderful state of Wyoming, when he told me that the old-timers in the highway patrol used to refer to it as no-man's-land because of the interference from the two-thousand-foot granite walls of the canyon that used to make radio contact all but impossible — and the legend of this particular Highwayman was born.

First off, I need to thank the Wyoming

Highway Patrol's Captain Jim Thomas — I just hope he likes his new nickname.

Jackie Dorothy of the Wind River Hotel & Casino and denizen of the canyon was also irreplaceable in her knowledge of the area and the Arapaho. She's the one who put me in touch with wordsmith James Andrew Cowell to make sure my Arapaho wasn't too terribly bad.

Some of the research materials I was fortunate enough to obtain were the *Arapaho Stories, Songs, and Prayers* by Andrew Cowell, Alonzo Moss Sr., and William J. C'Hair and the Hot Springs County Pioneer Association's *Mystic Wind River Canyon.*

My usual riding partners were in on this one, "Gale-Force" Gail Hochman and Marianne "Motorola" Merola. The folks down at headquarters, Kathryn "Command Central" Court, Brian "Where the Rubber Meets the Road" Tart, "Lucky" Lindsey Schwoeri, "Victorious" Victoria Savanh, Ben "Buggy-Bath" Petrone, Angie "Mess with the Best" Messina, and Marcus "Ridin' on the Rim" Red Thunder.

And lest I forget, because she would remind me, Judy "Shotgun" Johnson, my love and companion in all things in this world and the next.

1

There is a canyon in the heart of Wyoming carved by a river called Wind and a narrow, opposing, two-lane highway that follows its every curve like a lover.

Traveling north through rolling flats, there is a wind-scoured, rocky terrain that stands like a fortress next to the shores of the Boysen Reservoir with icy water that reflects the Owl Creek Mountains, looking as if they might split the continent in two.

At this point, there are three living-rock tunnels that enter the canyon in a row — rough, incongruous, like the passages that my mind still races through from the time when both I and the interstate highway system were young. Once out of these vintage boreholes, surrounded by granite walls towering 2,500 feet on either side, there are some of the most ancient rock formations in the world.

The Precambrian cliffs glowed pink in the

late-afternoon sun that peered over the tops to illuminate the road signs that note the geologic history of the canyon, once again making me feel as if I were falling through time.

I figured that's what she was doing, standing at the edge of one of the overhangs that dropped down into the turgid water.

I'd parked my truck at one of the pull-offs that bulge out from the road so that the tourists can get a better view of the Wind River. By federal treaty, the Shoshone and Arapaho are the only ones allowed to outfit white-water and fly-fishing ventures in the reservation portion of the canyon, and there were a few of these brave individuals navigating rafts and drift boats through the fallen boulders and jutting rocks that populate the foaming, churning waves. At the Wedding of the Waters, the river changes its name and magically becomes the Rocky Mountain Bighorn River as it speeds north, almost as if the Wind could not survive in the white man's world.

I was surprised to find her here at all, standing on the ledge below, barely visible in the drifting mists. She looked the way I remembered her from our many interactions in my county, tall and angular with one of those profiles that are hard to forget.

She didn't have her hat on, so her blond hair trailed back in the slight breeze, making it look as if she were moving instead of standing still.

My friend Henry Standing Bear was talking to his contacts on the Wind River Reservation in my truck, so I'd gotten out and had trudged to the edge of the canyon in the early-morning fog that had settled in the passage and would stay there until the sun reached its zenith to burn the great mystery away.

Decades earlier, close to fifty bighorn sheep were reintroduced to the canyon, first transported in horse trailers and then flatbed cars on the Burlington Northern line that runs along the other side of the river. The animals are still there along the crags when the cloud cover is not too low, like pale, solitary sentinels keeping an eye on the white water of the Wind before it escapes the gorge.

She leaned forward, looking at the cliffs on the other side, and I started to run, feeling that sharp shock as I realized she was preparing to jump. "Hey!"

She stopped moving but didn't turn toward me.

Afraid she might not have heard me, I shouted again. "Hey!" The sound of my fog-

15

muted voice echoed off the rock walls. "Hey . . . Hey . . . Hey . . ."

With a slow arc of my hand, I waved, and she turned her face to look at me but gave no indication that she recognized or even saw me. She just stood there.

Route 20 runs some thirty miles through the Wind River Indian Reservation from milepost 100 in the tiny town of Shoshoni to milepost 134 just north of Thermopolis, home of the world's largest mineral hot springs. In good conditions it can take as little as forty minutes to drive the Wind River Canyon Scenic Byway, and in bad, it can take a lifetime.

"I'm not crazy, Walt."

"Nobody is saying that you are."

We sat there in her spiffy Dodge Charger and watched the traffic thread its way through the canyon on a cold April morning. The fog had cleared a bit, and we could see where the late frost had caressed the aspens, the chartreuse buds still glowing with an unearthly desire for life. Every once in a while a few husks would break loose, would catch the breeze, and then flip through the air before they fell onto the frigid surface of the blue-black river.

"They're wanting me to go in for a psychi-

16

atric evaluation." She laid an arm on the sill of the Wyoming Highway Patrol cruiser and focused her eyes on the traffic like a blond-haired hawk.

"That doesn't necessarily mean they think you're crazy."

She studied the road. "Have you ever been called in for one?"

Usually it's the weather that impedes travelers who attempt to navigate the narrow canyon, snow that chokes the tapered passage like a mountain pass, drifting so that the highway disappears, or clouds that descend and fill the gorge like a funnel, rolling down the highway as if it were a tsunami, just as blinding and inevitable.

Then there is the wind for which the canyon and the river are named, howling whistlers of over forty miles an hour that shoot their way through the tunnels, singing an end song that dies over the whitecaps of the reservoir, a sound that no human can hear.

I glanced over at Rosey Wayman, who was rolling a large coin between her fingers. Tall and blond, lean and mean, she had blue eyes like searchlights that set you back when she looked at you. I'd known her for more than a few years when she'd been assigned to the Highway Patrol division in our part of the state. Through a few mutual cases, I'd observed her and come to the conclusion that she was one of the best HPs with whom I'd ever dealt.

"How long have you been in this division?"

"Troop G?"

"Yep."

"About three months now."

There was a call that came through from down near Shoshoni, the town south of the canyon, and we both glanced at her radio. "When did it start?"

"The first week."

"Every night?"

"No."

"But the same time each night?"

She sighed, and I watched as she stopped rolling the coin. Some of the tension left her body as she realized that finally somebody was taking her seriously. "Yes."

"Standard frequency?"

"*Our* frequency, 155.44500 RM."

"What time?"

"12:34 a.m." We looked at each other, the two of us aware of the importance of that particular time around these parts.

"You mind if I ask you a different kind of question?"

She shifted in her seat and turned toward

me, giving me all the blues I could handle as she went back to rolling the coin over her knuckles. "Go ahead."

I gestured toward the mist-swept cliffs ahead of us, the vibrations of the falling water still discernible in the cruiser. "Out there on the edge of the cliffs, when I called out to you and you first saw me — why didn't you answer?"

Sometimes it's the rockslides that surprise the tourists, the state geologists, and the Wyoming Department of Transportation, unsure as to how they could've happened at all — things that may not impede travelers but certainly make their journeys more interesting, because the Wind River Canyon Scenic Byway holds a distinction unlike any other road in Wyoming.

She turned her head, placed a fingernail under the coin, and flipped it to me. I caught it in my right hand and opened my fingers to look at it. "Because I wasn't sure you were really there."

I studied the silver dollar, which was in surprisingly good shape considering its age, and mused on the stories I'd heard my entire life. You see, the Wind River Canyon Scenic Byway is haunted.

Henry and I waited patiently as Kimama

Bellefeuille gave a blessing to the steaks sitting on the table in front of us. Kimama was an Arapaho medicine woman with a Shoshone name who gave the impression of being a thousand years old, and people generally did what she told them to do because she wore them down, like a glacier.

"Cese'éihii heetih-ceh'etii-n hióówo'owú-u."

The two of us were sitting together, our combined weight of over five hundred pounds on a single bench seat by the window in the restaurant while the ninety-pound, seventysomething-going-on-a-century-old woman on the other side of the booth had a bench seat to herself; it was a question of respect. Henry leaned toward me. "She is asking the animals of the earth to hear her words."

"He-ciiyowoon-inoo, heet-wonibiini-heetih-'iéhi-t."

"Your surplus is going to be eaten so that the people will prosper. . . ."

She interrupted him and said something I couldn't make out.

"What'd she say?"

"She wants to know if I am going to translate each line of the prayer." The Bear looked unsure, maybe for the third time in his life, and we both looked at Kimama like truants. "I thought that —"

Kimama interrupted him, and Henry translated. "She says she can continue in English for the Bird Turd, if you would like." He bit down on a grin and made the decision for me. "That would be appreciated."

"Umm, did she just call me a bird turd?"

He nodded and spoke through the side of his mouth. "Bird shit is generally white."

I turned back to Kimama, but she had already recommenced the prayer, this time in English. "So that the breath of life will endure for a long time, so that the tribe will be numerous, the child whatever his age, the little girl and the little boy, and man, whatever his age, and the woman, even the Bird Turd, whatever his age . . . We pray that these foods will keep us healthy as long as the sun follows its path in the sky."

Watching the old woman open her eyes and pick up her utensils, I figured the religious portion of the meal was through. "I don't like being called Bird Turd."

She mumbled something more in Arapaho, and I turned to Henry. "What?"

"Kimama says she will call you Frosty, if you prefer."

I looked back at the medicine woman. "I don't like that one either."

21

She mumbled something more before cutting a piece of her steak and forking it into her mouth.

"She says she will call you Niice'nooo."

"What's that mean?"

"Bucket."

"Why is that?"

Henry laughed. "Because you are beyond the pale." I stared at him. "Get it? Bucket." I continued to stare at him. "Pail?"

"No." I watched as they shared a glance and then began using my knife on my steak and not her. "Well, I'm going to call her Pain In The Ass."

She mumbled something more in Arapaho.

The Cheyenne Nation rolled up a forkful of pasta. "She says she has had that name since before you could drive."

"I bet she has." I ate a bit and looked at Henry. "What's she got against me?"

"I don't like big men."

I turned to look at her, envious of her easy switch from Arapaho to English. "Why?"

"Maybe I will tell you someday, Bucket." She studied me through her sharp, dark gimlet eyes. "So, what did the flat-hat say?"

"She said she wasn't crazy."

Kimama grunted, now working on her string beans. "You know, only crazy white people say that."

I sipped my beer, a Speed Goat from the microbrewery this side of the Bighorn Mountains in Ten Sleep. "So they tell me."

Her dark eyes came up. "Do you think she is crazy?"

"Nope."

She picked up a French fry and dipped it in ketchup. "There are spirits in the canyon, great spirits that one time formed the earth."

"I'm mostly interested in one in particular."

She cocked her head at me and chewed, and I could see every muscle in her face. "Maybe you will meet him."

"Have you?"

" 'Ine."

I sat my glass down. "I assume that means yes?"

She grinned, and you couldn't help but like the old broad. "You're learning."

"Was it a pleasant experience?"

"Helpful."

I stared at her, trying to convey the importance of the favor we were asking. "Will you come with us tonight?"

"I have a prior engagement. And besides, what you are asking is after my bedtime." Her eyes dropped, and she carefully cut another bite of steak. "But be careful what you wish for, Bucket."

We finished our meal, dropped Kimama Bellefeuille off at the Methodist bingo hall, and headed up the road to the Troop G Wyoming Highway Patrol headquarters in Worland, the small brick building looking like a mini fort stranded out in the frontier wilderness with only a lone pine tree outside. "Think she'll warm up to me?"

"I doubt it."

"Think we can get her to change her mind?"

"No, but we will give her time, just in case."

I paused before opening the door. "Do you mind if I ask why it is that she's so important?"

"It is *their* canyon."

"Actually, it belongs to the state of Wyoming."

"The Shoshone and Arapaho have prior rights, and since she is both Shoshone and Arapaho . . ."

I pushed the door open and shouted, "You decorate that tree out there at Christmas?"

Jim Thomas pushed off his chair and walked over to the counter that separated us. "No, but I put out a bowl of red and green M&Ms. That's about as festive as I get."

He was handsome, with a blond crew cut, pale blue eyes, and an easy grin. If the Wyoming Highway Patrol were to have a poster child, he would be it.

"Might appease the Natives."

He shook hands with the Cheyenne Nation and gestured for us to have a seat in the available office chairs. "I'm not sure anything will do that." Saying nothing else and leaving the proverbial ball in our court, he sat back in his chair and studied us.

"How are you, Jim?"

"Good. Glad to be off I-80."

"I bet. Congratulations on the promotion, Captain America."

He grimaced at the nickname, and I felt like telling him about my just-acquired one. "Thanks." He glanced at Henry and then back to me. "To what do I owe the pleasure of you being on this side of the mountain?"

"I got a call from one of your troopers last week."

He rested an elbow on the arm of his chair and palmed his face. "She called you?"

"I'm afraid so."

"What'd she say?"

"That you were trying to get her in for a psychiatric evaluation."

His hands dropped to his lap. "Wouldn't you?"

I glanced up at the wooden rack of mugs on the wall, a few of them blank but most of them adorned with not only the Wyoming Highway Patrol emblem but also the patrolman's name. "Has this ever happened down there before?"

He sighed and stood, going over to the counter again and leaning on it with his muscled arms folded. "Not that I'm aware of. I called Mike Harlow to try and talk with him, but he hung up on me."

The Bear looked at him. "Who is Mike Harlow?"

"The trooper who had the Wind River Canyon patrol up until three months ago, when Rosey took it over."

I chewed the inside of my lip. "And who had it before he did?"

"Bobby Womack."

We all grew quiet at the mention of the man's name. "Why do you suppose Harlow won't speak to you?"

"Probably because he's sick and tired of talking about Bobby Womack." Thomas slid a hand along the old Formica. "Mike's a little sore. I think he was hoping that they'd give him command of G, just as a figurehead for a few months before he retired." He sighed. "But they brought me up, and I think he got a little pissed off."

"Do you think it would make a difference if we asked?"

"Maybe."

"Where is he?"

"He retired and bought a cabin down in the south end of the canyon. You can't miss it — he's got a Marine Corps flag on a pole down there."

I raised a fist. "Semper Fi." I lowered my hand and eased back in my chair. "Kind of odd, retiring in the place he patrolled for all those years."

Jim nodded and smiled, his face looking even more like that poster child. "We all thought it was pretty odd. I asked him about it at the little party we had for him the beginning of February, and you know what he said?" The big captain shook his head, the close-cropped hair not moving a bit. " 'Nobody ever gets out of that canyon, so I'm not even going to try.' "

We sat there for a while, listening to the radio chatter from all over the state. "What do you think it is, Jim?"

"I wish I knew. Rosey's a sterling officer — that's why I invited her over when I got the command — but this thing's got me licked. I don't know what to make of it. I sat with her down there in that car, and we never heard a thing; three nights I did it. Nothing."

"She says it doesn't happen every night."

He spread his hands, truly at a loss. "And what am I supposed to do with that, Walt? I've got a wife and two daughters. I can't just go down there and sit in the canyon with one of my troopers. That's why I have them, to do the jobs that I can't."

"Still, you've heard the stories."

He looked at the rack of mugs on the wall. "Yeah, I've heard 'em. We've all heard 'em, haven't we?"

"Yes."

The trooper turned his head, surprised that the Bear had been the first to speak. "All the way up on the Cheyenne reservation?"

"The moccasin telegraph never sleeps."

Thomas stood and walked over to the mugs on the wall, including one with his own name. "You see these? There's one for every trooper in G, past and present." He pulled his own from its cubby and twirled it on his finger like a six-shooter. "When a trooper dies, we turn his mug toward the wall, solid white."

I studied the rack. "Which is Bobby Womack's?"

He touched one at the upper left-hand corner. "This one right here."

"Can I see it?"

"No."

I glanced at Henry. "Do you mind if I ask why?"

He filled himself a cup from the urn and leaned against the counter. "When I first got here, every once in a while . . . not every day, but every once in a while, I'd come in and that mug, Bobby's mug, would be turned back around to where you could read his name."

"So why can't I look at it now?"

"I superglued it down." He turned and rinsed his mug in the adjacent sink and then carefully dried it and put it in its cubby just below Womack's. "You know what they call him?"

"Heeci'ecihit." The Bear leaned back and laced his long fingers in his lap. "That is what the Arapaho have always called him. Heeci'ecihit — the Highwayman."

2

"His mother liked the R & B singer. She had one of those console record players, and she used to play Sam Cooke and Bobby Womack albums all the time, so she named her only son Bobby." The dreadfully obese Arapaho man shook his head. "Since the singer's name was Womack, she thought they must've been related somehow. Couldn't ever convince her otherwise, especially after he did a country album."

"Is she still alive?"

"Oh no, long dead. I think sometime back in the eighties."

"Are there any Womacks still around?"

"There's an aunt, I think, over in Fort Washakie, but I'm not sure exactly where. She'd probably be in her nineties by now." Sam Little Soldier smiled. "Hey, I heard you had lunch with Kimama — how'd that go?"

I shrugged. "She's calling me Bucket."

He studied me. "You are kind of beyond the pale."

"So, Bobby was the first Arapaho trooper?"

"The very first of the people to become a flat-hat, yes. It was quite a stir for a while — he was about as famous as Sacajawea around these parts. There were a lot of people who were offended by it, though, said he'd gone over to the other side, but Bobby, he was just like that — always helping people."

"So, you knew him pretty well?"

He nodded. "We went to school together."

"Where?"

Sam gestured to the area around his office. "Right here. They started Central Wyoming College up in 1966, and Bobby and I got in in '68 when they were still having classes in the basement of a bank downtown. We both played basketball for the Shaman and then transferred down to Laramie."

Henry raised an eyebrow. "The Shaman?"

Sam nodded. "That was the name of the sports teams before they changed it to the Rustlers."

"I think I like 'Shaman' better."

Sam laughed. "Yeah, me too, but we got too many First Nations/Indigenous Peoples/

Aboriginal Americans/Natives around here to go for that."

"Was Bobby tall?"

He shook his head. "No, he was a little guy, but one of those bundles of baling wire and tough as hell." The three-hundred-pound man reached over his shoulder, pulled down one of the numerous black-and-white photos on his wall in the Wyoming Public Radio office, and handed it to me. "Front and center, holding the ball, the one with the black socks. He was one of the most gifted power forwards I've ever seen. He was fast, too fast for all these corn-feds around here. Played on dirt his whole childhood, barefoot. Then the high school came along and gave him shoes and a wooden floor? He was unstoppable."

First I studied the younger and much thinner version of the man in front of us and then the young Bobby Womack sitting in the photo, a dark swatch of hair covering one eye with the other taking all comers, looking into the camera and maybe the world. "What happened in Laramie?"

"Some guy from Arizona State side-checked him and that's when his knee went; walked with that limp the rest of his life. He finished his degree, though, and we all figured he'd teach and maybe coach somewhere, but that's when he put in with the Highway Patrol."

Pulling my eyes away from the young man in the photo, I looked at his friend. "With a bad knee?"

Sam laughed and parts of his anatomy jostled to join in. "Yeah, even with a bad knee he outdid everybody at the academy."

I handed him back the memories. "Hard to believe."

"Yeah, well . . ." He set the photo on his desk and studied it. "That was Bobby." A moment passed, and then he glanced at Henry, finally resting his dark eyes on me. "So, why are you two world shakers down here asking questions about Heeci'ecihit?"

I smiled. "So, you know the legends?"

"Oh, yeah. The Highwayman of the Wind River Canyon . . . Tribal story. After the incident, the old women would threaten their children with him." He stuck out a fat finger and shook it at me. "You don't do what you're supposed to, Heeci'ecihit will come and get you!" He laughed. "Bobby would've loved that — he was one of the worst kids on the rez."

"What changed him?"

Sam chuckled. "He grew up — every once in a while it happens — been there, done that. Hell, you know as well as I do that

33

young outlaws make the best lawmen." He studied us some more. "But you still haven't answered my question, and I'm wondering why you would come down here and start asking people about old ghost stories."

"Jim Thomas says you're the local radio expert around these parts."

He shrugged and gestured to a silent young man with bristling black hair who now stood in the doorway of the office. "It's my job supervising the station, but it's his passion. He knows more about radios than I ever will. My grandson, Joey."

"Is that true?"

The athletic-looking college student nodded but kept his eyes to the ground. "I do a lot of ham radio stuff, and I've pretty much got a radio museum at home."

I leaned forward, taking my hat from my knee and running the brim through my hands. "Okay then, how hard would it be to break into the Highway Patrol's radios?"

He looked at me strangely, his eyes finally finding mine. "You mean the frequency?"

"Yep."

He thought about it. "With the proper equipment, not very hard at all, but you can get into a lot of trouble doing that shit." He glanced back at his grandfather and then between Henry and me. "So, what's hap-

34

pening?"

I smiled. "Do you know Rosey Wayman, the new HP in Troop G up in the canyon?"

"The blonde?" He registered a smile at my surprise at his knowing her. "There aren't that many of them around here and anyway, she's flip."

I glanced at Henry, my go-to guy for youth speak.

"Hot."

I turned back to Joey. "She's been hearing things on her radio."

He looked uninterested. "What kind of things?"

"She says she hears Bobby Womack."

Joey didn't move for a few seconds but then turned to Sam. "Is this a joke?" He stared at the Cheyenne Nation for a few seconds more and then turned back to me. "Tell me this is a joke."

"I wish I could — she says that every night or so she hears him on her radio in the canyon. It's to the point where her captain is ready to send her in for psychiatric evaluation."

"He should."

I was a little taken aback. "You're not curious?"

Sam stood and interrupted. "About what? That she's hearing radio transmissions from a guy who's been dead for more than thirty years?" He turned back to Henry — apparently the interview was over.

Joey stepped back, clearing the way, and spoke to the Cheyenne Nation. "I can't believe that you're doing this." He gestured toward me. "After what they did to Bobby?"

"Wait, who did what to Bobby."

The young man crossed his arms over his flat stomach. "Jim Thomas, he didn't tell you that story, huh?"

"What story?"

He took a deep breath, calming himself, and then looked at the photo on his grandfather's desk. His fingers came up and covered his mouth, and his eyes narrowed to black slits. "Maybe you should hear it from somebody else. I'm kind of biased."

I waited, but then Henry stood and rested his hand on Joey's arm. "Then could you tell us, Sam?"

Sam looked at the man in the photo again and weighed whether he was going to share. "Hookuuhulu, don't you have basketball practice?" The young man made a face, pushed off the doorjamb, and retreated without a word. "C'mon, I've got another appointment, but I'll tell you the story on the way to the parking lot."

He gathered up a battered briefcase and a

coat, and we followed him through the hallways and out an exterior door, where a vintage blue import sat behind the main building.

Henry was the first to ask. "You have still got this thing?"

The large man placed a hand on the fender. "This is my baby."

I studied the car. "What is it?"

His hand glided up and down the fender. "This is the very first Japanese import into the United States market, the Toyopet Crown. It's actually a Toyota."

"It is actually a piece of crap."

"Like you're a judge." The heavyset man frowned at us. "Not to change the subject, but back to the stories — you ever heard of the 1888-O 'Hot Lips' Morgan silver dollar?"

"I've heard of the Morgan silver dollar."

He leaned against the very compact car. "Back in the early sixties there were stashes of the Morgan, the most famous coin of the Old West, that got released from some long-forgotten government vaults, and the Treasury ran onto a bunch from the New Orleans mint that had been double-struck in error, which resulted in a doubling up of Lady Liberty's lips, nose, and chin — hence the moniker 'Hot Lips Morgan.' "

I fished out the coin that Rosey had flipped to me in the cruiser and tossed it on the hood of the car in front of him, where it landed flat but vibrated in a circle on the metal, finally coming to rest. "Look like that?"

He pulled out his reading glasses, guiding them onto his face, reached out with his free hand, and peered at the silver dollar. "Where did you get this?"

"Rosey Wayman gave it to me."

He smiled. "They went up for auction, and a portion of the find ended up in storage at the Central Bank & Trust here in Riverton, headed for some collector in Helena."

"I'm assuming they never got there."

"No. There were a couple of fellas who worked for the Wyoming Department of Transportation and one of them part time as a janitor at the bank, and he figured a way to get into the basement and steal the damn things, ferreting them out little by little until they had more than a thousand."

"Wow."

He picked up the coin and stared at me. "The bank was getting wise to them, so they lit out north and got as far as the canyon, but when they were pulled over, both of them got killed, and the bag of Hot Lips Morgans was gone."

"Who pulled them over?"

He rested a hand on the car. "Who do you think?"

"Bobby Womack."

Flipping his ponytail back and resting his hand against the side of his face, Sam studied the coin. "There was a big to-do, and a lot of suspicion fell on Bobby from both sides."

"Why?"

"The two WYDOT guys who stole the Hot Lips Morgans were Indians and known to Bobby." He shrugged and as he climbed in the clown car, its suspension crouched down on one side. "Everybody figured it had been some kind of inside deal with Bobby in on it, and when things went bad Bobby decided to divest himself of his two partners."

"Did he have any history of that kind of thing?"

Sam slammed the door of the car, barely getting it closed, and began cranking the starter a few times before it caught. He started to back away, but the import stalled. "Not once."

"Then why would anybody suspect him?"

Sam Little Soldier continued to study the silver dollar in his hand before tossing it back to me. He cranked the uncommunicative engine of the Toyopet Crown again and then sighed in the silence. "Because he was an Indian."

Static. "I've never heard that story."
I keyed the mic with the radio preset to Jim Thomas on the HPs frequency. "Probably before your time, you pup."
Static. "That's Captain Pup."
"Right." I glanced at Henry, who was staring through the windshield of my truck as Trooper Wayman had a conversation on the side of the Wind River Canyon Scenic Highway with a motorist in an aged Diamond Rio tanker truck that she had pulled over. "Right. Anyway, can you get me the reports on the incident so I can check it out?"
Static. "Happy to. So, you guys are settled in for the night?"
"Yep."
Static. "Well, I'll be listening up here, but Rosey says it's a faint signal, so if it does happen I probably won't hear it."
I checked the clock on my dash. "We've only got a half hour to go."
Static. "Give me a report in the morning."
"Roger that."
Static. "Hey, Walt?"
"Yep."

Static. "If you don't hear anything tonight? Well, I'd really appreciate you helping me get her to talk to someone. I'm really worried about her."

I keyed the mic one last time. "Right."

The Bear studied Rosey, who was still engaged with the trucker. "If she does not give him the ticket soon, she may miss her call."

I pulled the Morgan from my jacket pocket. "We can take a message."

He reached out and took the coin from my fingers. "What did she say about this?"

"She didn't. I was hoping to hear more tonight."

He gestured through the windshield. "Well, it looks as if you are going to get your chance."

The running lights of the truck Rosey had pulled over disappeared into the distance as she walked past her unit, yanked open my back door, and climbed in. "I hate that rat."

"Who?"

"Coleman. He owns a crappy heating oil business in Thermopolis and runs the fuel down to the rez during the winter at jacked-up prices. I've charged him a couple of times, but I can't get anything to stick." She glanced over the seat at the dash. "What time is it?"

"A little after midnight."

The Cheyenne Nation chimed in. "And only six days till Easter."

Rosey slumped forward onto the back of my seat with a sigh. "This may be the longest half hour of my career."

The Bear held up the silver dollar. "Care to tell us about this?"

She looked at the two of us, reached up and took the coin, and then delved into her duty shirt pocket. Pulling out an identical Morgan, she handed them both back to Henry. "That's the second one I've found."

"Where?"

She leaned back in the seat and looked at the headliner. "The first one was near mile marker 117 about two and a half months ago. I was driving down from Thermop right at sunset, and there was something gleaming on the road. I pulled over and stopped, and there this thing was, sitting in the middle of the two painted lines like somebody put it there."

I took the first one from Henry and examined it. "Well, that's kind of funny. . . ."

"That's not the funny part. About eleven that night a Jeep Cherokee hauling three kids from on the rez blew a tire and swerved, rolling the thing against the inboard rock wall at the exact spot that the coin had been."

Henry's voice rose from the darkness on the other side of the cab. "Did any of them survive?"

She nodded. "The two passengers did, but the driver was dead on scene when I got there."

The Bear held up the other silver dollar. "And this one?"

"About a month ago I found it at mile marker 115 at the same time of day, right when the light gets really perpendicular, you know? That last little bit of light that hits everything and makes it stand out? I was driving along, and I saw something flash in the middle of the road so I stop, and sure as anything that coin is laying out there shining like a beacon."

I traded Morgans with the Cheyenne Nation and studied the second for any signs of wear, but there were none, and the silver dollar looked as if it had just been double-minted down in New Orleans. "Then what?"

"Nothing."

"Nothing?"

"I check back there less than an hour later — nothing. I sit there for another hour, and it starts raining, so I call myself every stupid

43

name in the book and head north. I catch this idiot on a Harley about twenty miles over, up near the fly shop, and pull a quick U-ey, run him down, both of us standing there in the pouring rain; some lawyer from Colorado and he's all Do-You-Know-Who-I-Am, so I give him the citation. I turn around and head north, you know, finishing my loop, but I get this funny feeling."

"Yep."

"So, I flip around and head back down, but there's nothing there, so I pull up and park. It was a slow night and nobody was out, so I just sat there for a few hours waiting to see if anything was going to happen." She glanced out the side window. "Nothing."

"Well, that proves that it was just —"

"The next day at around noon there's a message on my cell phone from Captain Thomas saying some kayakers found this guy and his Harley over the cliff, smashed up by the water." She continued gazing out the window into the darkness. "The medical examiner said he probably survived the fall but was broken all to pieces, laying down there on the rocks all night while I was sitting right above him, you know, watching the road and looking for ghosts." She finally turned her head, and I could see the small reflection in her eyes. "Mile marker 115, right where I found the second coin."

There was a blip on the radio as another patrolman reported in from Shoshoni.

Static. "Unit three, 10-7."

"That's Parker, out of Riverton. He's got a bladder the size of a grape."

I considered the coin. "You know the story about Womack and the Central Bank & Trust theft?"

She studied me. "You think I haven't looked up everything there is to know about him?"

"Then you tell me."

She unzipped her jacket and took off her hat and tossed it on the seat beside her. "I haven't read the official transcript, but I checked out all the newspaper articles in Thermop and Riverton. It was a righteous shooting. He pulled these renegade WYDOT guys over just north of the tunnels and one of them had a shotgun, blew out the windshield of Womack's cruiser. He planted in a one-two position and shot the guy in the chest before he could reload the 12-gauge. The passenger was out by then and fired over the top of the car with a snub-nose; now, you know as well as I do that unless you're locked in a phone booth with a perp those things are pretty useless, but the guy hits Bobby in the side, busting a rib. Womack returns fire — one shot, right in the head. Two assailants, two men dead on scene."

"And no bag of Hot Lips Morgan silver dollars?"

"Nowhere to be found."

"They go through the car?"

"Took it completely apart in a garage in Worland. Nothing."

"Did they search the canyon?"

She laughed. "It's twenty miles long, Walt. You could hide an entire town up in here and nobody would ever find it."

"Yep, but you said the shooting took place just north of the tunnels, as did the two coin incidents."

"So?"

"So, that means that if they were heading north, they would've only been in the canyon a couple of miles before they met Womack."

"Yeah, but everybody's been scouring that end of the canyon with metal detectors since 1979. Again, nothing."

The Cheyenne Nation asked in a low voice, "Do you think Womack took it?"

"No idea." She studied him. "I mean, it's convenient, you know?"

"But none of the silver dollars have ever been recovered?"

"Not till about two and a half months ago."

We both looked at her.

"One at a time."

Henry handed his Morgans back to her. "Womack was killed about six months later?"

"Yeah, how did you know that?"

"Kimama, the Shoshone/Arapaho medicine woman, told me."

"He tried to stop an eighteen-wheeler that had lost its brakes. The driver was having a heart attack, and Bobby pulled out in front of the guy, I guess trying to slow him down as he went into the tunnels. Nobody knows why he decided to do something crazy like that, but the truck hit him sideways and drove him into the opening, punched him all the way through to the other side."

There was another radio call from Shoshoni.

Static. "Unit three, 10-8."

The trooper looked through the windshield, her eyes steady. "12:34 A.M. I hope he died quick and didn't burn to death. . . . You know, they say you could feel the concussion all the way across Boysen Reservoir."

3

"So, you didn't hear anything?"

I adjusted the Bear's cell phone on my ear and spoke to Jim Thomas again. "You've got a trooper with an irregular bladder."

"Yeah, Parker. We try and keep the duty meetings short when he's in attendance." There was a pause. "You sticking around or heading home?"

"We thought we'd stay one more night just to see if there's anything to it. Hey, Jim, do you know anything about the Central Bank & Trust Hot Lips silver dollar heist?"

There was a pause. "The Hot Lips what?"

"Just some ancient history. We'll get back to you if we find anything."

"Right."

I hit the red button on the screen and handed the phone back to its owner. "Never heard of it, so you can tell Sam Little Soldier's grandson Joey to take a powder."

Henry pursed his lips. "As you wish."

I studied him. "Something?"

"The young man is very angry."

"We used to be angry, too."

"I suppose so." He looked up at me. "What are you doing today?"

"Don't you mean 'we'?"

"No." He pointed at a blue van that was pulling up beside us in the Paintbrush Inn parking lot. "I am going rafting, and knowing your aversion to white water, I assumed I was going without you."

"Well, you're right about that."

I slid out and shook hands with a wide man in the driver's seat of the van. "Walt Longmire."

He smiled broadly, a grin so wide that I thought he might swallow his ears. "Dave Calhoun."

"You Shoshone or Arapaho?"

"I'm a Sho-Rap." He grinned again.

I turned back to the Cheyenne Nation. "He'll be too busy fighting with himself to drown you."

The Bear made his way around the front of the van. "What are you going to do?"

I saluted in a jaunty fashion. "Have a Marine Corps reunion."

"Be careful." He climbed in the van, which was towing a bright yellow inflatable raft, and they sped away to their fate.

I leisurely circled Thermopolis to take in the town, then swept back onto Route 20 and headed south, tacking through the switchbacks, just enjoying the drive. It was one of those crisp Wyoming spring mornings that made you feel sorry for anyone who lived anywhere else. There were a few snowdrifts up high where last night's low-flying clouds must've unladed themselves, but the pastures were still showing bright green, the juniper trees almost black in the morning light.

I'd asked Rosey if she'd heard the radio calls the two nights she'd found the coins, and she'd said that she had, but that she'd heard them on numerous other nights too with no coins attached.

I'd asked her why she hadn't tried to record the calls, but she'd said she had tried with an old cassette recorder, but all that came through was static.

Jim Thomas was right; it wasn't particularly hard to find Mike Harlow's place at the southern end of the canyon with the eagle, globe, and anchor on full display.

The Marine Corps flag carried ashore by Captain Samuel Nicholas onto New Providence Island in the Bahamas in 1776 was likely the British/American hybrid Grand

Union Flag, but it's also possible that it was the GADSDEN DON'T TREAD ON ME. A more indicative version arrived in the 1830s with the anchor and eagle and the words TO THE SHORES OF TRIPOLI, which changed to FROM TRIPOLI TO THE HALLS OF MONTEZUMA after the Mexican-American War.

I parked the Bullet in a spot to the side of the driveway, which was blocked by a reinforced gate locked into two concrete pillars. On each side of the gravel road, a steel fence with three-inch pipes stretched as far as I could see in both directions.

I stepped up onto the second rail of the gate and swung a leg over, landing on the other side.

By the time the Corps hit the beach in Vera Cruz in 1914, the flag was blue, with a wreath encircling the globe and an anchor emblem at the center with two scarlet ribbons and the words U.S. MARINE CORPS above and the motto SEMPER FIDELIS below.

I glanced around and gazed up the road with a steep terrain that swept to the right and then circled to the left, disappearing in the juniper trees, where I assumed there was a cabin.

There was a period during World War I

51

when fringe and inscribed battle honors were sometimes attached to the flag, but an order in 1925 put an end to such shenanigans, and in 1939 the official colors of scarlet and gold were adopted as the Corps standard, resulting in the flag we have today.

I paused to salute both the Stars and Stripes and the current version of the Marine Corps standard, along with the smaller guidon beneath it. This guy was seriously gung ho.

When I reached the turn, I took a breath and could see a small cabin built out of river rock notched between two very large boulders. Swiping my hat off, I wiped away a little sweat and started up again as a voice barked at me, "That's close enough."

I stopped and peered into the shadows of the porch and two partially open windows and noticed a thickset man with a light-colored cattleman's crease cowboy hat and Vandyke facial hair the color of coal; he was sitting on a swing with a rifle propped up in his lap.

I raised my hands in mock surrender. "Howdy."

He didn't move. "Go away."

I dropped my hands. "How about a little western hospitality."

"No."

"Are you Trooper Mike Harlow?"

He took a few seconds to think about it. "Who are you and what do you want?"

"Walt Longmire, sheriff, Absaroka County. I was wondering if I could ask you a few questions."

"About?"

"It might be a wide-ranging conversation; would you mind letting me come up and sit on that porch while we talk?"

He didn't say anything, so I took that as an invitation. I approached the house, stepped up on the wide-planked deck, and sat down in an old wicker chair, which was barely big enough to hold me.

He eyed me with the butt of the weapon still resting on his knee. "Careful, I'm armed."

I nodded. "I can see that. You mind putting the safety on that Red Ryder BB gun?"

He shook his head and studied me through a pair of Ray-Bans. "Cocked and locked, that's just how I roll."

"You'll put your eye out."

"That's why I've got these safety glasses." He adjusted the Wayfarers again and pointed the barrel of his weapon at a collection of bird feeders in the junipers between the boulders. "Damn magpies won't let the little wrens eat, so I'm on watch."

I smiled. "Third Battalion, 9th Marines?"

"You read my flags." He cocked his head. "You?"

"1st Marine Division, Military Police."

"When?"

"Vietnam."

His head lolled back on his neck. "Good, you were before my time, so you probably didn't arrest me."

"Not unless you committed a homicide."

"Investigator? You must've been one of the first."

"I was."

"You here because of the magpies?" He gestured with the BB gun. " 'Cause I haven't got a license, but I haven't hit one yet either."

"I'm here because of Rosey Wayman."

"That one of my ex-wives?"

"She's the patrolman who took your duty in Troop G."

"The blonde?"

"Yep."

He slipped off the sunglasses and studied me for a long while with sharp blue eyes. "You made the climb — you want a beer?"

"I thought you'd never ask."

He turned the Morgan silver dollar I had handed to him over in his hands.

"You never found any of these on the road?"

"Nope, wish I had. Hell, this thing is like new."

"Make you wonder?"

He lowered the coin and sighed. "Why is this important to you?"

"I know Rosey, and I think there must be something to it." I propped the BB gun on my knee the same way that he had. "You worked this canyon for over thirty years; I find it hard to believe with all the stories flying around that you never had anything strange happen."

"Did I say that?" He sighed again and then sipped his can of Coors. "That poor bastard ain't ever gonna find peace. Every time things die down about Bobby, something else happens."

"Did you know him?"

"He was my training officer."

"Was he a good TO?"

"Better than I was as a trainee." Harlow leveraged himself up from the swing and walked past me to the porch steps. When he leaned on one of the support posts, I watched it give a little. "He was about the best I ever seen; smart, patient, good-hearted but no pushover. He was tough, really tough." Harlow shook his head.

"Inhumanly tough." He turned his back against the post and rubbed the way a bear would. "One of the first stories I heard after he died was one from these tourists out of Iowa. They came up here in early October in their short pants and T-shirts in this old sedan with bald tires on their way to Yellowstone. People think the thing is open year-round."

He sipped his beer as I sighted in on one of the large black and white birds. I pulled the trigger and watched as the BB arced out, falling well short of my target.

"You've got to pump that thing four or five times or it won't make the reach. Hell, I think I can throw a BB harder than it shoots. Doesn't hurt the damn things, but it teaches 'em respect."

I pumped the Red Ryder and took up my position again. "What happened with the tourists?"

"Oh, we had one of those high-plains clippers come through and dump a few metric tons of snow in the canyon back in '91 and they blew a tire and then slid off the road. It was really coming down, and they were in the middle near Windy Point. Well, it wasn't like they could change the tire or hike out in the clothes they had, so they just sat there."

I took aim on another magpie. "With the motor running."

"Yeah, and after a while they all start getting sleepy, but there's a knock on the window and someone standing there, real close. It's a trooper in one of the long black slickers with his hat pulled down so that you can't see his face. The dad rolls down the window, and the fellow asks if they need some help. The dad says yeah, so the trooper goes around, pulls out the spare and jack, changes the tire, and sends 'em on their way."

Sensing the oncoming shot, the magpie ducked and swooped down the canyon. "Uh-huh."

"They take a wrong turn and end up in Worland, and the dad sees the Troop G headquarters and decides to stop in and tell 'em what a great guy we've got in that trooper that helped 'em out in the canyon. So the captain asks him which trooper, figuring it was me, and the guy says he doesn't know 'cause the trooper never introduced himself. Then he remembers that when the patrolman told 'em they could go, he'd seen the name tag on his slicker." Harlow sipped his Coors and fingered his Wayfarers down on his nose. "Womack, Bobby Womack."

Another magpie lit on the feeder, and I re-aimed. "Twelve years after his death." I pulled the trigger and fared better this time, knocking the big bird from the perch as he shrieked at us and disappeared over the porch roof.

"Nice shooting there, Tex."

"Could've been carbon monoxide poisoning."

"Yeah, it could've been." He crossed back over and took his seat in the swing again and rested the beer on the railing. "Then there was this hitchhiker, hippie kid out of Benicia, California, who was heading north and got picked up by a trooper in the canyon really early one morning and said he gave him a ride all the way up to Canyon Hills Road and dropped him off. The kid wanted to buy him a meal to thank him, but the trooper said there was something he had to take care of but if the kid wanted to buy him lunch, he knew a place and would meet him at the end of the road in about an hour."

"So?"

"The kid does what the trooper tells him to do and goes out to the end of Canyon Hills."

"And?"

"There's nothing out there but Monument Hill Cemetery."

I didn't say anything.

"Where Bobby's buried."

I rested the Red Ryder in my lap for lack of targets. "You ever have anything strange happen to you?"

He thought about it for a while, watching the smaller birds come in and take advantage of the magpies' absence. "Back in 2000, WYDOT was painting the center strips, and we had to ride along in front of them, straddling the line so some idiot didn't come around a corner and run into their trucks. Well, I'm pulling the duty, and we stop at the Tipi Camp about halfway for lunch, and one of the crew comes up and asks me to say something to the trooper who's running behind us. According to this guy, he's got his windows down and has been playing the same song over and over and would I please do something about it."

I sipped my beer. "And?"

"Well, I tell this idiot that there isn't any other trooper, that I'm the only one on duty in the canyon, but he keeps complaining, so we walk back there and of course there's no other patrol car. Now, normally I would've just let it drop, but I was curious, so I asked him what the song was."

"Yep?"

"Said it was that old Rolling Stones tune 'It's All Over Now,' and that he must've heard it about forty-seven times."

"So?"

"You know who wrote that song?"

"Nope."

"Bobby's namesake — Bobby Womack." There was a long pause as he looked out to his right toward the byway. "Strange stuff, I shit thee not. I used to let it prey on my mind a great deal, but I just got to the point where I stopped. I figure things are going to happen, and a lot of them are going to be unexplainable."

" 'There are more things in heaven and earth, Horatio, than are dreamt of in your philosophy.' "

"Meaning?"

"There might be a lot more going on around us in this world than we're aware of."

He handed me back the coin. "Amen to that, brother."

I pocketed it. "Do you think he did it?"

"Stole that money?" His eyes unfocused, and he sat there looking at nothing. "Hell, no."

"Then why did he do it?"

"Do what?"

"Pull out in front of that runaway tanker

truck and kill himself?"

He got up again and walked back over to the same post, leaning against it, and I noticed it was rubbed smooth. He must've spent a lot of time standing there, looking at the road below, the opening of the north tunnel just visible in the distance. "Bobby drove this big ol' LTD with a 460 Police Interceptor motor in it; he used to turn the lid on the air cleaner upside down, you know, high-school shit. . . . Man, you would hear the *wump* of that thing when he got on it — sounded like a rocket ship." He drank some more beer. "There isn't a month that goes by that I don't swear I hear that damn thing goin' up or down my canyon."

4

"I was born here."

"In the canyon?"

Rosey took her eyes from the road and turned to look at me. "Riverton."

"I never knew that. I thought you were from near Cheyenne."

"We moved there when I was four."

"Really?"

"Yeah, my father worked for the phone company, and they kept switching him around all over the country. Mom's mind is starting to go and I'm not sure how much she remembers is real, but she says I had a nanny in Riverton that I used to call Butterfly, but I don't remember anything like that — don't remember any of the time we spent there, but I was four. I guess when we moved to the big city, I just forgot about the place."

It was a slow afternoon, and it seemed strange that she was in civilian clothes. We'd gone out for a late lunch but had been drawn back to the canyon. She wasn't on shift for another couple of hours, so we sat in my truck and stared at the turbulence, hoping to get a glance of Henry and the other crazy man in the rubber raft as they white-watered by.

I was reluctant to bring up the subject of why Henry and I were here, but knowing that unless something miraculous happened tonight we'd be heading back over the mountain tomorrow morning, I spoke up. "I had an interesting conversation with Mike Harlow this morning."

"He talked to you?"

"He did."

She nodded, returning her eyes to the water. "How did you accomplish that?"

"I went to his cabin."

She shook her head and licked her lips, the gray light of the overcast day flattening her refined features. "He doesn't answer his phone or have e-mail. I even wrote him a letter, but he never answered and I finally gave up. It never occurred to me to just walk up his driveway — seemed intrusive."

"It was, but he didn't shoot me."

"Did you show him the silver dollar?"

"I did."

"And?"

"He'd never seen one. I mean, he knew the story, but he'd never found one on the road like you."

"What about the radio calls?"

"He says in his entire thirty years in the canyon, he never heard one." We sat there in the silence of my truck and continued to watch the water. "So, when these calls happen, what do they sound like?"

Her eyes didn't move, but her jaw stiffened and she pulled the handle and climbed out, quietly closing the door behind her. I sat there for a few moments, giving her time to collect herself, and then got out, rounding the front of my truck, where we both leaned against the grill guard.

She kept her personal blue searchlights on the water, traveling north through the canyon. "This isn't me, you know? I've never had anything like this happen to me in my life, and I guess I'm not dealing with it really well."

"I think you're doing okay. If I had dead people talking to me on my radio every night, I'm not so sure I'd be completely rational about it either." That at least got a smile. "I've had strange things that I can't explain happen to me, Rosey, so I think I know a little bit about how you feel."

She turned to look at me. "So, you're

haunted, too, huh?"

"I think we're all haunted, by one thing or another."

"Glad to hear it."

Far in the distance, I heard a familiar whoop, and we both turned to see the two aquatic braves fighting the rapids with all the gusto of a war party. Dave Calhoun was in the back, digging in with two oars on either side of the rubber raft, while Henry kept switching sides, paddling with a single oar. The front of the raft lifted, but Henry continued to struggle as the float shot through a water funnel and turned sideways toward a large boulder the size of an automobile.

Rosey stepped toward the edge of the cliff. "Oh my God."

I shook my head, figuring there wasn't a lot I was going to be able to do if they crashed into the thing, except possibly fish for parts.

The Bear dug in and turned the front of the raft toward the right side of the boulder as Dave paddled like a steamship, attempting to get them to the side of the rock before they hit it.

Fortunately, the central current caught the raft and shot them alongside the boulder. They flew underneath us around the next corner, but not before the Cheyenne Nation turned our way and, throwing up his hands, screamed at the heavens, "Howou-unoni — yehewihoo!"

The sound of the Bear's voice reverberated off the rock walls as they disappeared, and she turned to look at me. "Do you think you have to be crazy or Indian to willfully do that sort of thing?"

"Maybe to enjoy it." We listened as the battle cries grew distant, and I figured they'd made it. "So . . . what does he say?"

"Who?"

"The midnight caller."

She walked back to my truck. "He calls in a 10-78, officer needing assistance."

"Simple as that?"

"There is a loud static noise and then he identifies himself as Unit 3, which is my number. The first time I got the call, I answered and asked him if he was Troop G or belonged to a different detachment, and if he wasn't, who was he and how can I help?"

"Then what?"

"Nothing for a few minutes, and then he repeated the call, identifying himself as Unit 3 and once again calling for a 10-78."

"Did you try and talk to him anymore?"

"I did."

"And?"

"Nothing, he just repeated it again."

"Verbatim?"

"Yes."

"Could it be a recording?"

"No."

"Why?"

"There are slight variations in the cadence, tone, things like that."

"How do you know it's Bobby?" She looked at me again. "Hey, I'm an investigator — I'm investigating."

"There are audio recordings of him at the library in Shoshoni. I went and tracked them down — heck, some of them are on the Internet. It's him, Walt, I'd swear to it."

"Do you know Sam and Joey Little Soldier at the college?"

"No."

"Sam teaches down there and Joey's his grandson — Sam knew Womack and his grandson appears to be an expert on the man."

"You think either of them would come up and listen?"

I watched the clouds topping the canyon walls. "I think we better get some corroborating evidence before we try and draw a crowd." I waited a moment and then asked a more philosophic question. "So, are you saying that he's still alive?"

She slipped off the glove with the pearl snap and bit her thumbnail. "I don't know."

I stuffed my hands in my jacket and attempted to be a voice of reason. "Bobby Womack is dead, Rosey."

"You know, the legend goes that the Indians arrived here after crossing the great sea of the Big Horn Basin, and the land was so big that it made it impossible for the people to find game, so they prayed to the Creator and asked him to help. He did, by draining the sea and catching the water and the fish and game in the narrow canyon, and the people were saved." She stared at the ground and didn't move. "But what if that isn't all that got caught? What if there's a little bit of Bobby left here in the canyon, too?"

"Why now?"

She finally looked at me, a strong lock of blond falling over one eye. "Exactly."

"I talked to Vic and Ruby back at the office and they said to tell you they were glad you didn't drown."

"Tell them thank you for me." Henry sat on the bench outside our motel room and wrung the water from his socks. "How was your conversation?"

I continued to peel my apple with my old Case Russ-Lock. "Which one?"

He draped the socks on a nearby planter, which somebody had filled with pansies in a desperate attempt to hurry the season, and leaned back against the wall. "Let us start with the first."

"Mike Harlow seems like a pretty good guy — I hiked up to his cabin. He's just gone hermit and doesn't respond to phone calls and e-mails." Cutting off a piece of apple, I chewed.

"Sounds like somebody else I know." He stretched his legs out, his toes grabbing at the sun-heated air. "Had he had any strange experiences?"

"A few, over the years." I sat on the bench at the other side of our door and related the stories that Harlow had told me earlier.

He sat there unmoving. "No radio calls or silver dollars?"

"No."

He nodded and thought. "Why would there suddenly be more incidents of a supernatural nature in the canyon?"

"What do you mean?"

"Thirty-five years after the death of Trooper Bobby Womack and only a handful of incidents since. Why would things appear to be happening with a greater frequency now?"

"Rosey was just asking me that same question."

He grinned that hidden little smile he did when he knew something you didn't. I got that smile a lot. "As she should — what *is* the one thing in the canyon that has changed?"

I rested my chin in my palm. "Rosey."

"Yes." He stretched his shoulders, unbunching the knots that had collected battling the rapids. "So, the situation begs, is she simply more susceptible to the influences of Bobby Womack than someone like Mike Harlow, or is she somehow personally connected?"

"I don't see how. She says she was born down in Riverton, but her family left when she was four, so they couldn't have known each other." I stood and walked out into the April sun, warming my shoulders after the seemingly endless winter. "I don't see how they could've ever met."

"How old is Rosey exactly?"

"I don't know, but we can ask Captain Jim, because I'm not asking her. I've done some crazy things in my life, but asking women their age isn't one of them."

"Is Mike Harlow from here?"

I thought about the man's accent. "I don't think so. Pennsylvania maybe? Why?"

"Having been born here might make Rosey more susceptible to the ways of the canyon." He frowned. "Does she have any Indian blood, specifically Shoshone or Arapaho?"

"Not that I'm aware of, I mean, she's blond-haired and blue-eyed — maybe she's Cherokee?"

"You know what you get when you have sixty-four Cherokees in one room?"

I glanced at him sideways. "One Indian. I'll tell you this much, if somebody other than Rosey doesn't hear Bobby Womack on that radio tonight, then all this is going to come to a screeching halt."

"What does the spectral trooper say?"

"He identifies himself as Unit 3 and calls in a 10-78." I noticed the Cheyenne Nation's blank look and felt foolish; I assumed that with all his dealings he'd absorbed everything I knew. "Officer needs assistance."

"And that is all?"

"Yep." I readjusted my hat and turned to look at the passing traffic on the road leading toward the canyon. "It's strange, because why would he be calling for backup? The man died pulling his cruiser directly in front of a runaway tanker truck — it wasn't like anybody could've helped." Tipping my hat back, I ran the calluses on my hand over my face. "But there are other types of assistance. We're taught to work independently, but nothing strikes you quite like a 10-78, the urgency to reach a fellow officer in need. It's instinctual to individuals who are trained to respond and risk their lives for each other and complete strangers." I spoke through my fingers. "But what if it's a psychological cry for help?"

"Meaning Rosey again?"

"Yep. Look, I don't think we're going to hear anything on that radio tonight, but what if what Rosey is hearing is what she wants to hear or, more important, what she needs to say?"

"Hmm . . ."

"There's such a stigma attached to this type of thing, and it's rampant in the line of work, and whether you call it crazy or not it's hard for a cop to make that call on themselves."

"So you do not believe?"

"No."

"What about the instances that Harlow mentioned?"

"All explainable. The flat-tire incident could've been caused by carbon monoxide poisoning from the occupants sitting in a running car in a snowbank. Heck, they're lucky they didn't die of asphyxiation. The hippie hitchhiker? Who knows what he was on. The WYDOT guy working in the sun too long with some random driver following the paint truck and playing the same song over and over again — it's all explainable."

He gave me the smile some more. "Yes, it is, and one of the simplest explanations is one you seem to be incapable of entertaining." Then he reached out and took the rest of my apple.

We sat on the tailgate of my truck in front of the grave and studied the ribbons tied to the sagebrush near the headstone, the medicine bundles and assorted objets d'art that had been left by the two tribes of the Wind River Reservation.

"It's a shrine."

"Yes, it is."

I started picking out different things on the grave at Monument Hills Cemetery. "What's the meaning of the broken arrow to the Arapaho?"

"Peace."

I pointed to a small stone carving.

"In most Native cultures, the wolf is considered representative of courage, strength, loyalty, and success at hunting and is big medicine. The origin stories of some Northwest Coast tribes, the Quileute and the Kwakiutl, tell of early peoples changing from their wolf forms to that of men."

"Why are wolf fetishes white?"

"Among the Pueblo tribes, wolves are considered one of the six directional guardians associated with the east and the color white. The Zunis carve stone wolf fetishes for protection, ascribing to them both healing and hunting powers."

I turned to look at him. "What about the Shoshone and the Arapaho?"

"In their mythology, the wolf plays the role of the noble creator god, or the brother and true best friend of the culture hero. There is an Arapaho legend concerning a white wolf and a woman."

"Okay."

"There was a beautiful woman, proud and independent, who wanted no man and painted her tepee herself. One night she woke up to find a man wearing all-white robes in her bed. It was dark, and she could not tell who he was, so she dipped her hand in the red paint by her bed and, as they made love, she held the small of his back, marking him where he could not see. Later, she looked for the paint on all the men of the tribe, but none of them were marked. She became pregnant and went into the forest to gather wood, thinking surely the father of her child would reveal himself. Suddenly a large white wolf ran from the trees and stood in front of her. The woman was very afraid and raised up a piece of wood, ready to strike the wolf, when she noticed the red handprint on the wolf's back. Angry at what people might think if they found she had slept with a wolf, she brought the limb down and killed it. Later, when she arrived home, she saw that the tepee flap was undone and there was blood in the entrance. Still holding the stick, she pushed the flap open and entered, finding the most handsome man she had ever seen sitting in the back with a bandage wrapped around his head."

Silent for a while, we sat there at the end of Canyon Hills Road and listened to the wind. "So, he was the wolf."

"No, he was the sun."

"I don't get it."

He nodded, thoughtful, his eyes focusing on the distance. "If you were Arapaho or Shoshone, you would."

5

"This is shaping up to be a really bad day."

"Why?" Henry and I were sitting on the tailgate of my truck again, but we'd changed locations and I'd treated the three of us to a pizza and a six-pack of soda.

We were backed in tail to tail, Rosey sitting on her trunk lid with her windows down and her radio turned up. She took a bite, washing it down with a root beer. "My car wouldn't start."

The Cheyenne Nation groaned. "Oh, no."

"Yeah. I got dressed, came out, and hit the starter — nothing. So, I call the service station guy we use, you know, and it takes him an hour to get there, and he jumps it and it fires right up."

"Battery?"

"That's what I thought, but he turns the thing off and hits it again and it starts on the first crank."

The Bear lip-pointed toward the Dodge.

"Sounds like some kind of short."

She nodded as she chewed. "I guess, but you guys aren't leaving before it starts. The last thing I want to do is spend the night down here, you know?"

I patted the file tucked under my leg. "Thanks for the folder on Bobby."

She cocked her head. "My pleasure. As you might well imagine, he's kind of become a preoccupation. Besides, you should have plenty of time to read tonight."

We hadn't seen another car in about an hour. "Traffic gets a little sparse after nine o'clock, huh?"

On cue, the monstrous, rusted, dangerous-looking oil truck that had passed us before rattled down the road headed south with no tail or running lights.

"Well, damn."

"Let it go."

She placed her slice back in the box, sat the pop next to me, and started for the driver's-side door of her unit. "No, if somebody slams into the back of Coleman Fuel, it's not going to be on my watch."

"You want one of us to ride along?"

She shrugged. "If you want — you don't get enough traffic stops over in Absaroka County?"

Henry gave me a nod, and I slid off the

tailgate and dropped the rest of my slice in the container too, taking my root beer and the file with me. "Don't eat all the pizza while we're gone."

He glanced down at the box as I slid into the cruiser. "What pizza?"

Rosey hit the ignition, and thankfully the Dodge fired up. She slipped it into gear and hit the light bar, swung onto the empty road, and jetted after the unlit truck.

We caught up in a couple of minutes; of course, the driver was reluctant to pull over, though I can't imagine there were many options for flight in the battered truck. Finally, he turned into the pullout near the first tunnel before you get to the Boysen Reservoir.

Rosey hit her dash cam and radioed in the plate numbers before easing out, slipping on her signature leather search gloves with the pearl buttons. I sat there for a moment but then put my soda can in the holder and got out on the passenger side, unsnapping my Colt and moving along the guardrail opposite her. I figured better safe than sorry as I approached the old Diamond Rio tanker truck that I pegged as being from the fifties.

The conversation was already getting heated as I looked up into the passenger window of the beater, noticing a padded pistol case on the dash and a certain tang in the air. "You wanna tell me why you pulled me over this time?"

"I need your driver's license, registration, and proof of insurance, sir."

"You know my name, missy." He waited and then added, "And what if I don't have it this time?"

"I'll have to impound your vehicle, at which point you can call somebody to come and get you."

"How many times are you and me gonna do this shit, huh?" He grumbled some more, then leaned up on one haunch and pulled his wallet from his back pocket. "You know, this country's goin' to hell in a hand-basket when you can't do anything without papers."

I watched as she studied the card in her hands with the Maglite. "Registration and proof of insurance, Mr. Coleman?"

There was a pause. "Haven't got it with me."

She turned the beam of the flashlight on the side of his face and studied him. "Mr. Coleman, have you been drinking?"

"Oh, now, horseshit."

"Would you mind turning off the ignition and stepping out of the vehicle?"

"Yeah, I mind." He sniffed and didn't

move. "I'm getting pretty tired of this harassment, you bitch."

She stepped back, still keeping the flash-light beam on him. "Mr. Coleman, I need you to step out of the vehicle."

"Look, I'm just going to the dump."

"At ten o'clock at night?" He jumped at the sound of my voice, and both haunches came off the seat this time as he stared at me with his mouth hanging open. "Turn the ignition off and get out of the vehicle like the trooper told you."

I watched as his eyes flicked to the un-zipped soft case on the dash and then shifted back toward me and my 1911 on the sill.

"Suspended license, still no insurance, a half dozen unanswered citations, and who knows who the truck belongs to." With Coleman fuming in the back of her car, Rosey and I sorted through the front seat of his vehicle and collected the empty gin bottle and the S&W 29-10 .44 Magnum revolver that was in the soft case. "I've pulled him over about a dozen times now on assorted infractions, and he just gets worse each time."

"How long till the tow truck gets here?"

"They said about an hour, maybe longer since it takes a special wrecker to haul this monster."

"Same guys who fixed your car?"

She shut the driver's-side door and continued writing on her aluminum clipboard with the nifty self-lighting pen. "Yeah."

"An hour seems to be their standard response time."

She sighed and looked up the road. "I could have him at the Hot Springs County Jail, booked, and be back here in an hour."

I pulled out my pocket watch and looked at it. "Do it."

She glanced up at me. "What?"

"Run him in, and I'll babysit the truck." I took the Womack file with me, shut the passenger-side door, and leaned on the powder orange front fender of the Diamond Rio. "Stop and tell Henry where I am. If he gets bored he can come down here and get me."

"I don't want you to have to do this."

I pocketed my watch and glanced back toward the first of the narrow canyon entrances, the rough edges of the rock reflecting in the moonlight. "I've never been down here on foot — it'll give me some time to look around and read the reports."

She tucked the clipboard under her arm, straightened her hat, and handed me her Maglite. "You'll need a reading light. I'll be back in an hour." She pointed a finger at me. "Don't get run over."

I smiled and then waved as she pulled out, heading north at a brisk pace. I turned and looked at the tunnels.

It was the twenties when the state started thinking of a serpentine roadway that would replace the rough, steep grade of Bird's Eye Pass. At over 2,500 feet, the old road was open only part of the year and took several hours to traverse even with good weather.

That winter the mercury touched thirty degrees below zero, which enabled the engineers to cross the frozen river from the railroad tracks so that they could survey the terrain. The roadbed would be twenty-four feet wide, with hundreds of thousands of cubic yards of granite to be moved, culminating in a trio of eighteen-foot-wide, fourteen-foot-tall tunnels with a cumulative length close to a thousand feet.

I walked toward the north one, and it felt like the thing was opening in the darkness like a mouth, even eerier with the road completely vacant.

It was one of the most difficult engineering feats in the entire American West and expensive for the period. Work began June 1, 1922, and it would cost around half a million dollars but, all told, would prove to cost a great deal more than that. Lives were lost, some of the remains recovered after days and some never.

The insides of the tunnels weren't even in the beam of Rosey's flashlight, but I knew them to be rough like the surrounding cliffs themselves.

I stood at the narrow, red-painted curb on the right-hand side and looked up and down the winding road for traffic — there was none, so I stepped onto the roadway and walked to the center.

Tracing the beam up the road and then back to the tunnel entrance, I opened the file and looked at the printed copies of the newspaper accounts about Trooper Womack's last watch.

At 12:22 p.m., Officer Womack received a report that an eighteen-wheel tanker was traveling through the canyon and was carrying nine thousand gallons of aviation fuel to an airport in the southern part of the state. It was reported the driver was experiencing problems with his brakes and that he had already forced a number of other vehicles off the road. It was also noted that the truck driver was possibly experiencing a heart attack at the time.

It wasn't noted why Womack hadn't responded to the radio call by heading north and meeting the tanker. Instead he sat in the same spot where Rosey had just stopped Coleman, right outside of the tunnel itself, until the swerving eighteen-wheeler appeared at the far end of the S-curve only a quarter of a mile away.

I shone the light in that direction and couldn't help but feel a slight shudder at the thought of his seeing all nine thousand gallons of rich-mixture, 130-octane fuel heading for him at breakneck speed, most likely with a dying driver at the wheel.

Why?

Why sit there in the pullout, wait till the thing was almost on top of you, and then casually pull the LTD in the way. Why not just let the thing crash into the tunnel and explode? It just appeared an act of total, utter, hopeless self-destruction.

I walked in, shining the flashlight beam through this tunnel into the gaping maw of the next, which was only about a hundred feet farther.

The report states that with the impact the LTD was driven sideways before being pushed out the southern end and then had lodged itself along with the tanker truck into the solid granite buttress of the northern entrance to the second. The explosion had been tremendous, with fireballs racing from the ends of all three tunnels and the open spaces between. Campers at Boysen Reservoir thought that it must've been an earthquake, and legend had it that plate-glass windows had broken in Shoshoni, twenty miles away.

The heat of the blast had melted the road, and very few remains had been found, but the granite tunnels had miraculously held. After the accident, the inside surfaces of the tunnel walls were painted white on either side, but the ceiling was still black, with strange patches of concrete showing at uneven intervals.

I continued walking and ran my hand over the stone, the walls weeping even in this high desert, and I thought that if I were to touch the wetness to my lips it might be salty like tears.

The thrashing of the river was omnipresent, a noise that washed the canyon clean, amplified by the rock walls in front of and behind me. But there was another noise underlying the sound of the Wind, rock against rock where the animals of the night danced out their nocturnal appetites, some lucky enough to survive till daylight and some not.

I was walking the hundred yards in the open between the first and middle tunnel but about halfway became aware of a set of footfalls coming from the tunnel behind me and another coming from the one ahead.

I stopped, standing there in the clear spring air, with the glittering stars peering down on me, and laughed as I tucked the file and flashlight under my arm and thought about a grown man being haunted by his own footsteps echoing from two tunnels. I stood there listening and finally heard a noise to my left, where, as my eyes adjusted, I could see a great horned owl sitting in a stunted and still-leafless cottonwood that was attempting to grow in a fissure of the granite hillside.

"You getting scary in your old age, too?"

His head turned, and he looked at me with those radiant gold eyes as I listened to my words rebound a couple of times and laughed a response. "Well, I guess I am."

It was a cold night, and I flipped the collar up on my old horsehide jacket, slipped on my shooting gloves, and started off again, listening to the trio of six cowboy boots in cadence.

I stopped at the granite wall where Womack had most certainly died if he hadn't already been dead on impact. The stone wall traveled up like a keep, the first fourteen feet painted white, the rest stretching to a cold and forbidding darkness that extended into forever.

I took a deep breath and then billowed the vapor from my lungs like a locomotive gathering steam and pushed off again. The second tunnel was shorter, and a sudden bit of starlight glistened on the macadam roadway on the other side of the darkness. I picked up my pace, figuring I didn't have much time to get back to the entrance of the first tunnel before Rosey picked me up and we rendezvoused with the Cheyenne Nation to listen for the radio call.

I thought about what I was going to say when it didn't happen again. Henry and I, like Captain Thomas, had lives and couldn't spend our nights sitting in patrol cars waiting for phantom calls that never came. Wayman was going to have to talk with someone, someone who understood the things she was going through, and not just a couple of hard rollers like Henry and me.

I sounded tough, especially for a guy who had had his own run-ins with unexplainable phenomena, but I had rationalized all those things to myself and they didn't bother me near as much as they used to. Nonetheless, I raised my hand and fingered the large silver ring that I wore around my neck on a chain, the one with the turquoise and coral wolves forever chasing each other.

I approached the last tunnel and noticed the curbs on this one were painted yellow, different from the others, and wondered if they had run out of paint. Still listening to my boots echoing off the rock amplifiers in front of and behind me, it was almost as if I could hear a slight disparity in the rhythm, probably because of the difference in distance between the tunnels.

As an experiment, I stopped suddenly, and only a few footfalls echoed after me. Satisfied, I took up walking again and entered the third tunnel. I stopped in the middle, thinking that I should really turn around and get going. It was about then that I heard them again, just within earshot, footsteps my exact tempo — and I hadn't moved.

"Hello?" My voice bounced back at me, a query mocking my imagination.

There was no answer, but the footfalls receded as I turned and began running back in the direction I'd come. With the pounding of my boots on the roadway, I couldn't hear the footsteps any longer, but I didn't need to. I'd heard them for certain this time and was bound to at least catch a glimpse of whoever else was there with me.

Winded, I stopped in the middle of the second tunnel and looked around. I couldn't see anyone but could still hear someone else, running as I had been.

"Hello?" There was only the echo of my voice bouncing about from all sides as I lurched forward, yanking out the Maglite again and flashing it into the last of the tunnels just ahead — back to go.

It seemed as if there were something crouched down in the middle of the road, but I couldn't be sure. Picking up speed, I got closer and pulled my sidearm, causing the Womack file folder to fall out and scatter onto the roadway, the slight breeze pushing the sheets of paper like long-dead leaves.

I was right where whatever it was had been when I slipped on something, fell hard onto the pavement, and rolled to the curb. There was a roar as a vehicle in the tunnel blew past me, headed south. I lay there for a moment and then, rolling into a sitting position on the curb, I looked at the receding taillights of the car, just another midnight motorist headed home to Shoshoni or Riverton.

I shined the flashlight beam back to where I'd tripped — I could swear it was as if someone had been in the middle of the road in a hunter's crouch — but how had whatever it was escaped being run over by the passing car? Shaking my head, I gathered the pages that had scattered across the entirety of the tunnel and stuffed them into the folder, none too gently, annoyed with myself for behaving like a rookie and almost getting run over for the trouble.

I limped toward the open air when my boot hit something on the road's surface again. Cursing the night, I lifted my foot and looked down to see what I'd slipped on reflecting between the centerlines of the road. I knelt just as the figure had and picked up an 1888 Hot Lips Morgan silver dollar.

6

We sat there in Rosey's cruiser at the pull-off about a hundred yards from the entrance of the north tunnel and watched the giant tow truck pull away with the Diamond Rio tanker.

Henry had driven the Bullet over to meet us, and we'd been there for about forty minutes. The conversation had dwindled to the point where we all just looked at the green numbers on the dash clock as they ticked ever so slowly toward the appointed time, the unmentioned silver dollar burning a hole in my shirt pocket as if it had a circulatory system of its own.

The Bear's voice rose from the backseat. "How, exactly, did you hurt your leg?"

I'd had to use Rosey's first-aid kit to patch up my ankle — evidently, my explanation hadn't been satisfactory. "I tripped on the curb trying to get out of the way of a car that was going through the tunnels." I glanced at them. "I figured I had plenty of time before Rosey got back, so I thought I'd stroll down to Boysen Dam, but it took longer than I thought, so I decided to pick up my pace and head back, and that's where I met the car."

"In the tunnel?"

"Yep."

"Did you see anything else?"

I cleared my throat. "Um, not really."

Rosey had been listening but went back to watching the dash. A moment passed, and then she cracked open her door and climbed out. "We have another twenty minutes, so I'm going to grab some air." She walked toward the guardrail, placed a boot on the metal, and, leaning both arms on a knee, watched the dark water through the rising mist.

"You are a horrible liar; fortunately, she does not know that."

I turned in my seat to look at the Bear. "Yep, well . . ."

"What really happened?"

Static. A familiar voice crackled over the airwaves. "Unit 3, Walt? Anybody out there?"

I glanced at Rosey, but she hadn't moved, so I plucked the mic from the dash and keyed it. "Roger that, Captain America.

Isn't it past your bedtime?"

Static. Jim laughed. "Yes, it is. I just wanted to check in and see how you guys were doing."

"We're good. Rosey's getting some air, and we're just sitting here drinking coffee."

Static. "She's not there?"

"Nope."

Static. "Good. Walt, like I said, this is it. If nothing happens tonight, you guys need to fold up the tents and head home."

"Are you trying to get rid of us?"

Static. "No, but I also don't want you wasting your time. If this all goes the way I think it is, I'm going to want Trooper Wayman in my office at eleven. Do you think you could tell her that?"

"Sure."

Static. "I really appreciate you guys coming over and helping out with this, but I think it's time we circled the wagons and took care of our own, you know what I mean?"

"We do."

Static. "Well, if you guys have a minute, stop by the office on your way out, and I'll buy you a bad cup of coffee."

"Only if you promise not to glue our mugs down."

Static. "Over and out of my mind."

"Roger that." I hung the mic back on the dash and turned to look at the Bear. "You were saying?"

"What happened in the tunnel?"

"You aren't going to believe me." Reaching into my pocket, I pulled out the coin and handed it to him through the open slider of the grate that separated us. He stared at it for a moment and then back at me. "This one is marred."

"Only because I happened to step on it and slip sideways, which, by the way, kept me from getting run over."

He looked out the window. "It was in the road like the others?"

"Dead center, between the lines. I was running and hit the darn thing, and it may have saved my life."

"Running?"

"Yep." I glanced around to make sure Rosey hadn't moved and, satisfied, I told him about seeing something in the north tunnel.

"A shape?"

"Yep, kneeling down where the silver dollar was."

"Kneeling, so it was human?"

"I don't know. . . . I think so. I mean, what else could it have been?"

"Why were you running?"

"My footsteps were echoing in the tunnels, but then I started hearing other footsteps — ones that didn't match mine. I heard them, and then I heard them running away, so I chased after the sound back to the north tunnel."

He grunted. "Where the shape was kneeling and placing this silver dollar on the road?"

"Yep."

He grunted again.

"What's that supposed to mean?"

"You have a guardian." He smiled at me through the grate, and I knew it wasn't the first time he'd smiled at a white man through bars. "The shape, form, whatever it was placed that coin at the centerline so that you would slip on it and prolong your life."

"You don't think that's a bit of a reach?" I turned in the seat to get a better look at him. "I'm not buying into the ghost thing just yet."

"All right, but whatever it was, it saved your life."

"You don't think it could've been just a random, chance kind of thing?"

"No. In my experience with the residents of the Camp of the Dead, they rarely act randomly or leave things to chance."

"That supposition still depends on the willful suspension of all critical, rational thinking and a belief in things that go bump in the night."

He continued to smile, to my annoyance. "So, you think it is giant raccoons who have found the bag of silver dollars and are leaving them in the middle of the road to what purpose?"

Suddenly the driver's-side door opened, and Rosey threw herself in; slamming it behind her, she pulled off her gloves and blew warmth into her hands. "Jeez, it's getting cold out there." She turned to look at us both. "What are you guys talking about? It looked pretty intense."

"Giant raccoons."

She turned to look at the Cheyenne Nation. "That's a new one."

I glanced at the dash and could see that we had another four minutes before showtime. "I'm getting my thermos out of my truck; anybody want a cup of coffee?"

They didn't answer, so I pushed open the door and limped over to where the Bear had parked the Bullet and fetched the battered Stanley with the stickers on the side that read DRINKING FUEL.

Shutting the door, I started my hampered travels back to the cruiser when I thought I noticed something at the side of the road, near the opening of the north tunnel, a dark shadow that faded away into the uneven surface of the granite wall as I turned.

I took a step forward, but whatever it was, it didn't reappear. I thought about limping over, but we were coming down to the wire. I opened the door of the Dodge and wedged myself into the front seat. Screwing off the chrome top of the thermos, I poured myself a capful and checked the time.

12:32.

Without taking her eyes off the dash, Rosey asked, "You decided to brew some fresh?"

I took a sip. "Two more minutes."

"See any raccoons?"

I turned and looked at him. "Maybe."

I have had some long minutes in my life. I couldn't decide if I wanted to hear the radio call or I didn't. I knew I didn't believe, but what was I going to do then? Rosey was going to have to be confronted, and there really wasn't anybody in a better position to do it than me. I figured I'd start slow and gentle, trying to get her to see the impossibility of the situation and that she was going to have to come to terms with the fact that there was a problem — the first step in getting it solved.

12:33.

That she was going to have to move past the stigma of psychiatric intervention and realize that it was a difficult job that sometimes took its toll in strange and unpredictable ways. There was nothing normal about a career in law enforcement, and the strains of making life-and-death decisions every day were bound to have an effect. If need be, I'd tell her about my own experiences on the mountain in the snow. It wasn't anything I'd shared with anyone else, but this was important enough that maybe I could get her to understand.

12:34.

None of us moved, and I waited a few seconds before sipping my coffee in as nonchalant a manner as I could muster under the circumstances.

Rosey reached down and turned up the volume on her radio to the point that the electric hum of random frequency crowded the inside of the cruiser, and I could feel it in the fillings of my teeth.

I fussed with the heat and then figured I'd ask again. "Does anybody want —"

"Shhhh!"

I stared at her but didn't say anything. Henry stuck a hand through the slider, and gave him my half cup of coffee.

Rosey still sat there looking at the radio.

I turned and looked at it, too.

12:35.

I didn't move, not wanting to give the impression that these types of things happened with split-second timing.

She glanced at me, but I remained concentrated on the dash clock. She took a deep breath and sat back in her seat, started to say something, and then changed her mind.

I waited till the next minute passed. "Is it usually on the dot?"

She nodded and turned away toward the door. "Maybe a few seconds after, but it's always 12:34." She opened the door again and got out, leaving it hanging ajar. "I need some air."

I glanced back at Henry, then got out with my thermos and cup and pulled his door open for him, leaving ours open as well so that we might hear anything that came in over the airwaves. "Well?"

Rosey had resumed her spot at the guardrail.

"Would you like me to speak with her?"

"No, it's my line of work."

He nodded, reached into his pocket, and handed me back the silver dollar. "I'm going to go get my greatcoat out of your truck."

I looked at the very unhappy and confused woman by the rail. "Yep, it might be a long night."

"How 'bout a cup of coffee?"

"You think I'm crazy now."

"Yep, most people take my coffee."

She didn't move. "I think I might be losing my mind, Walt."

"You're not losing your mind, you've just had a few strange occurrences that have put you off." I unzipped my jacket, reached under my shirt, and pulled out the large ring on the chain around my neck. "You see this ring?"

"Yeah?"

I examined the thing myself, the available light reflecting off the silver. "A little over a year ago, a seven-foot-tall Crow Indian gave this to me."

"Okay." She looked at me when I didn't answer. "That's nice."

"Yep, it was, especially considering he was dead at the time." She stared at me. "Virgil White Buffalo kind of came to my rescue up in the Cloud Peak Wilderness while I was chasing down some escaped prisoners, one of them a very bad man." I waited a moment before continuing. "I was hypothermic, concussed, and damaged in about a half dozen ways. I needed company, and help, so I guess I came up with Virgil. I had conversations with him, interacted with him . . . but I know he wasn't there."

"Where'd the ring come from?"

"I found it."

"Just like I found the silver dollars?"

The one in my pocket burned like a heated rivet. "Yep, something like that."

"So, what are you saying?"

I shook my head. "I don't think it's important what I'm saying — it's what you're saying."

"And what is it I'm saying?"

"Help."

Crossing her arms, she pushed her boot off the guardrail and turned toward me. "Excuse me?"

"Rosey, you are one of the finest police officers I know — smart, tough, thorough, instinctive, fair, independent. . . ." I gestured toward the towering granite walls that surrounded us. "Heck, most people wouldn't even have put in for a duty like this down here at the end of the world, especially with all the stories, myths, and legends that surround this place." I lowered my arms and looked at her. "But there's something wrong. Think about it, think about what he says — Unit 3, that's you. You're Troop G,

Unit 3. Then he calls in a 10-78, officer needs assistance."

She stood there looking at me but saying nothing as the wisps of fog tangled around our boots.

"You need assistance. I think that's what this is all about — you need help."

She yanked her head toward the river and started to say something, but I cut her off. "Rosey, everybody needs a little help once in a while, but I don't think you're capable of asking outright, so you came up with somebody else to do it for you. Bobby Womack."

She looked down at her boots and bit her lip. "So, you do think I'm crazy."

"No, I don't. Haven't I been clear about that?"

"You don't believe me."

"I think you're mistaken."

"Mistaken."

I dipped my head, trying to catch her eyes underneath our combined brims. "It happens; we're not perfect." I glanced toward the vehicles and could see the Cheyenne Nation, giving us plenty of space, patiently waiting by my truck.

"So, does he think I'm crazy, too?"

I turned back to her. "Hold on just a minute. I'll let him head back to the motel with my truck and then you and I can talk." Not waiting for a response, I limped over and handed the Bear my thermos and keys.

"What is up?"

"This is probably going to take longer than you're going to want to stand out here for, so why don't you head back to the motel, and I'll catch a ride with her to Thermopolis?"

He stashed the thermos in the Bullet. "Tomorrow morning?"

I glanced back — Rosey hadn't moved. "Yep, it'll take that long, at least."

"I will stick around a little while, maybe head over to the tunnels and see what I can see." Without waiting for a response, he turned, the duster trailing after him like monstrous bat wings as he walked past the cruiser and down the road toward the cave-like entrance. "Hang on to that silver dollar — it might be good luck."

"Two times over." I looked back and could see that Rosey, listening to the invisible river, had stepped across the guardrail and was sitting on the cold metal. "Hey, you're going to freeze your ass off." I crossed and sat beside her, facing the other way with my hat in my hands. "So, what do you want to do?"

She kept watching the fogged-over landscape. "I want to keep being a highway patrolman."

"Who says you can't?"

"Oh, Walt. They don't like crazy people with guns."

"You're not crazy."

She smiled a sad smile. "I used to think I wasn't, too." She stood and took a few steps onto the worn rock of the promontory that jutted out into the void. "You know, I've been an HP my whole life — I don't think I know how to be anything else."

"Nobody says you're going to have to."

Her back was still to me when she spoke again. "What would you do if they told you that you couldn't be a sheriff anymore?"

"Probably dance a jig." I stepped forward, pressing my legs against the guardrail and holding out a hand. "Hey, it's getting really cold out here. Why don't we climb back in that snazzy car of yours and drink the rest of my coffee and talk things over?"

Her head turned just a bit, and her perfect Nordic profile was set off by the whiteness of the fog, her flat-brimmed hat dipping at a dangerous angle. "You've been a good friend, Walt, and so has Henry."

I started to climb over the guardrail. "Rosey . . ."

And then she stepped off the edge.

7

I stumbled forward, fell over the guardrail, and landed on my hands. I scrambled to my feet and looked into the impenetrable mist. My first thought was to jump after her, but the Bear was a far better swimmer than I was. "Henry!"

No answer. I stood there for a second more and then shucked off my jacket and tossed my hat, sidearm, and pocket watch along with it. Taking one step forward, I shook my head at the absolute insanity of what I was about to do — and leaped.

There was a brief moment of weightlessness, but then all 250 pounds brought their weight to bear and down I went. Heck, for all I knew, there wasn't any water below me, and I was just jumping onto the rocks along with an already-dead trooper. I didn't have to wonder long, however, as I plunged into the Wind River and it seemed as though the 640 muscles in my body contracted to the point of breaking all 206 bones.

The shock of the cold paralyzed me for a moment, and there was an explosion in my chest that caused every bit of air to go out of my lungs, and all I could think was that I had made a very bad decision.

I broke the surface and gasped my way free. The current was unlike anything I'd ever felt, and I'd no sooner gathered a couple of lungfuls of air when the flat of my back struck a boulder and pushed all of it out.

Sputtering, I tried to grab hold of the rock, but its wet surface slipped through my hands and I was shot through a funnel and submerged again. This time my leg struck something solid as the current plowed me forward. I'd heard Henry say that you always wanted to keep your feet up and pointed toward the current so that they wouldn't get caught and you wouldn't drown.

Lifting them, I bobbed to the surface just in time to strike another boulder, but not hard enough to completely disorient me. It was black dark, and the only thing that showed was the phosphorescence of the wave tops being cut by the wind.

Something loomed just to my left that I kept my boots aimed toward, but try as I might, my legs collapsed under me as I struck a much larger rock. I pivoted to the right and again tried to grab onto the thing, but everything was so wet and my hands so frozen that I might as well have been trying to grab hold with flippers.

Another swell caught me, and I rode it forward with a few seconds of visibility, thinking I might've seen something to my right. I reached out and made a grab for whatever it was.

A log.

Great, I was going to drown like a water-logged rat.

Its benefit, though, was that it gave me a little buoyancy, and I was able to see where I was going. It slapped into another boulder and I almost lost my grip, but I held on as the damn thing pivoted, swinging me around and rolling over my head like a giant baseball bat.

I was beginning to question its advantages just as I started short breathing. As near as I could tell, my lungs were seizing up with the rest of me as my core temperature plummeted. I figured I had another couple of minutes before I would become so immobile that I would likely sink.

The log struck something on both sides this time, forming a bridge of sorts, and I was able to get my arms over it far enough to hold on. Kicking to the left, I caught purchase but then felt my right boot catch on something beneath the surface, something that moved.

I hoped it was Rosey. I shoved my face into the water and reached down between the two rocks that held the log. With my frozen fingers going numb on me, I knew I had only one shot. Hoping it wasn't just a packing blanket that had flown off a passing truck, I yanked with all my limited abilities.

I flew forward but was able to get my legs spread far enough to hold my position and drag whatever it was up against my chest.

Rosey.

Pulling her in close, I tried to lean toward one of the boulders, but when I did, my footing started to give way, and the fire-hose current attempted to shoot the two of us back into the middle of the turbulent river.

My muscles continued to seize, and I had no feeling anywhere in my body. It was just a matter of time before my legs collapsed and we'd be sucked into the black water for good — literally stuck between drowning and a hard place.

With the last bit of energy I could summon, I applied all the pressure I could in an attempt to get Rosey above the water onto the boulder to my right. I'd almost made it when my leg slipped through the chute and I could feel myself starting to go.

It was at that precise instant that I felt a talon grip the collar of my shirt and pull me against the current like some giant bird of prey, and I saw Rosey being draped on the boulder, where Henry Standing Bear held on for a couple of dear lives.

He held Rosey with his right arm, his left fully extended in an attempt to hold on to me, and I could see the exertion it was taking just to keep me from slipping away.

"Grab my arm!"

I fumbled my hands toward him, but they were too numb to be of any use. "Save her!"

"Walt, grab my arm!"

I tried to grip his sleeve but couldn't. "Get her out of here and then come back for me!"

His dark hair fell around his face only inches from mine, and he yelled back with his black eyes blazing, "You will not be here!" I felt the tug as his muscles bunched and, pulling me to the side with inhuman strength, he inched me against the current. It felt like a crane with steel cables was wrapped around my collar, dragging me toward safety.

I summoned the last vestige of energy to

stumble forward, landing in knee-deep water. On my hands and knees, I coughed a couple of pints out of my lungs and crawled toward the rocky bank, finally collapsing on the hillside. Lying there and looking sideways through the high weeds still holding on to their pale winter color, I watched as the Cheyenne Nation lifted Rosey onto his shoulder and trudged up the embankment, his duster coattails flowing out as if taking flight just before the two of them disappeared over the guardrail.

I rolled over onto my back and turned my head to cough up more water.

I lay there for a moment, feeling the intense cold of the fog. Finally finding a small pocket of reserve, I leveraged up on one elbow and gripped the stalks of grass in an attempt to get upright. Half making it, I stumbled up the hill, mostly on my hands and knees.

When I got to the guardrail, it seemed to soar over me like a landscape. Putting a shoulder against it, I pushed myself over, falling onto the other side, and just lay there like a drowned albatross. I rested my head on the back of a hand and saw the opening of the north tunnel in the distance.

We hadn't gone that far in the river, but it sure had felt like we had.

Raising my head and turning it a bit, I could see Henry about fifty feet away trying to resuscitate Rosey, his powerful hands laced over her chest.

I crawled toward them. It wasn't that I thought I could do much, but lending some moral support might make the difference. I made it about halfway there when everything gave out, and my nose hit the pavement like a pickax, the blinding flash of concussion almost enough to put me out.

Stretching my right arm, I kind of sidestroked like some half-assed hermit crab, making about eight inches a minute until I got near the rear of her cruiser. I think I blacked out, but I can't be sure. The back corner of the Dodge hung over me, but my eyes traveled down across the road to the entrance of the north tunnel.

Where a man stood looking at me.

He was dressed in some sort of uniform, and as he limped directly toward me, his fists at his sides, I could see he wore a flat-brimmed hat. The badges and decorations pinned to his dark jacket flashed underneath the black, rubber-coated canvas slicker. He wore dark slacks and highly polished boots that shone like mercury on the macadam.

He hobbled toward me, one boot forward, the other dragging behind, but Henry's ministrations on Rosey's behalf must have caught his attention, and he moved toward the front of the cruiser to look over the hood.

I watched him, trying to discern what his intentions might be, but then I got annoyed and yelled, my words mangled by my frozen lips. "Stay away from her!"

He turned.

"Stay away from her, damn it!"

He stayed like that for a couple of seconds, his profile burnished by the cruiser's interior lights, and then turned to look directly at me. It was the same face I'd seen in the photographs, only harder. I couldn't make out his eyes but was rapidly getting the feeling that I'd gotten the attention of something I might not live to regret.

"Bobby Womack."

He stared at me.

"You can't have her."

With one last glance at Rosey, he trailed a gloved hand over the sill of the open door of the cruiser and stepped out to stare at me. His head canted and, dragging one boot, he began to move.

"Go away." I automatically tried to reach to my side, but even if my hands would have worked, I remembered I'd disarmed myself before the jump.

In a couple of halting steps, he was standing over me. I tried to back away on my elbows, but he kept up and knelt down, bringing his face in close to mine.

The eyes were black, no white at all, just twin tunnels leading nowhere. He crouched there, just as he had on the road, and began working the glove from his fingers a tug at a time.

"What do you want?"

He paused for the shortest of moments and finally freed his hand. He held it to his face and blew into it just as Rosey had when she'd gotten back in the cruiser earlier tonight, but his breath was like a blast furnace.

Casually, he turned his palm and started reaching for my face.

I tried to draw back, but with no energy to defend myself, I flopped to the side and just lay there looking up at him.

He was about to reach out again when one of the Morgan silver dollars fell out of my shirt pocket and dropped onto the surface of the road. It rolled forward, circled once, and then, glinting between us, fell over flat with a metallic sound.

He stared at the coin with ebony eyes and then, extending a forefinger, he placed it on the coin, whereupon the surrounding asphalt began smoking with the stench of burning oil and tar. The coin glowed red and slowly sank into the pavement, and I'm sure it would've gone all the way to hell if he hadn't lifted the tip of his finger, blowing on it like the barrel of a fired pistol.

He glanced at Henry and Rosey. My eyes followed his, and I could see the Bear had her on her side as she retched the river water from her body.

When I turned back, his face was close, and I could feel the heat waves emanating from him.

He stayed like that for a few seconds, and then I became aware of his lips moving. The words were faint but powerful, like the canyon wind, and a smile traced itself to the corners of his eight-ball eyes. "Unit 3, 10-78, officer needs assistance."

I narrowed my eyes at him and tried to sit up but wavered a little, not wanting to get too close. "What officer needs assistance?" I scrubbed my hands over my face, but when I started to ask again, he was gone. Nudging an elbow beneath me, I sidled up and caught sight of the silver dollar that had fallen from my pocket. It was resting on the surface of the pavement — not seared into the melted asphalt, no burns, nothing.

Static. "Unit 3, 10-78, officer needs assistance."

I looked around for him again, but he wasn't there, just Henry holding Rosey up against his chest as she sobbed, the two of them looking into the cruiser, where the same voice that had just haunted me came from the radio, loud and clear.

Static. "Unit 3, 10-78, officer needs assistance."

8

I stared at the hands on my pocket watch. "The time was wrong in her cruiser — they never adjusted it after they jumped it, and that's why the clock was an hour slow."

"That is not the point."

I sat there, still trying to get warm after a shower and clean, dry clothes. "No, I suppose it isn't."

"You heard it, the same as I did."

Hot Springs County Memorial Hospital was a lot like the hospital back in Durant, especially the mauve waiting room with the mauve walls, mauve carpet, mauve drapes, and off-mauve furniture.

"It was exactly one hour late."

Leaning back on the mauve sofa, he attempted to get me to answer. "You are not addressing the question."

"Bear with me for a moment." I sat forward in my chair with the thankfully not-mauve blanket still wrapped around me, resting my elbows on my knees. "That means that the electrics on the cruiser went out exactly one hour before the service guy got there."

"Yes."

"Exactly sixty minutes to the second. Doesn't that strike you as odd?"

He laughed a gruff bark. "Yes, in the sea of odd that does strike me as a strange wave."

I gave him a dirty look, but it didn't appear to have any effect. "Yep, I heard it." He circled the sofa and sat facing me, willing to engage in conversation now that I had answered the question. "Does the fact that I was half drowned, delirious, and occasionally unconscious limit my credibility in this?"

"No, because I heard it and so did she."

Pulling the coin from my pocket, I slumped back in my chair and examined it for burn marks, but there weren't any. "How do you know that she heard it?"

"Because she was crying."

"How do you know that's what she was crying about? She'd just attempted suicide."

"They were tears of relief — I know the difference. She was crying because we heard it, too." He stood, stuffing his hands in his jeans and walked toward the hallway to see if anyone happened to be listening. "For the first time, someone besides her heard Bobby Womack's radio call."

"I'm not so sure that's going to count for much."

He turned to look at me. "What does that mean?"

"It means nobody is going to care, Henry. The only thing they might do is give us all adjoining cells at the psychiatric hospital down in Evanston."

He kept looking at me, and I watched as his jaw clenched. "Then we have work to do. Now that we know this is happening, we need to find out why."

Hearing someone coming down the hall, the Bear turned and walked to the window and stood there looking out with his back to the room.

Still clutching the blanket around me like Nanook of the North, I slowly got out of the chair as Cami Slack, the young doctor who had treated both Rosey and me, and Jim Thomas, who was wearing civilian clothes, entered the room. They were chatting between themselves but then broke off when they saw us.

"How's she doing?"

Dr. Slack ignored my question and came over for a checkup. She took my hands in hers, felt my pulse, and then on tiptoe pried open a lid and stared into my bloodshot eye. "She's all right, exhibiting secondary drowning symptoms — coughing, shortness of breath, chest pain, and general lethargy from water being in her lungs, preventing oxygenation. She'll probably be okay in twenty-four hours — well, we hope." She let go of my eye and put her fists on her hips, looking to me like she was twelve. "So, how are you?"

"Fine, how are you?"

She glanced at Jim. "Is he always like this?"

"Pretty much."

Turning back to me, she tugged at the front of my blanket. "Why do you still have this?"

"Because I'm cold; I am sure I will be cold till the next gubernatorial election."

She raised a hand and slipped it between my collar and my neck, and her fingers were nice and warm. "Cold water carries heat from the body twenty-five times faster than air, so once you go in, you immediately begin losing core temperature. Your body attempts to generate heat by shivering, but that's not enough to combat the monumental loss of heat to the water." She released me and turned to look at Thomas again, attempting to get an ally in ganging up on me. "What do you think the temperature in that river is tonight?"

"Midthirties, I'd say."

Shaking her head, she turned back to me. "Loss of dexterity in less than three minutes, exhaustion, disorientation, and unconsciousness in a few more. I'm just guessing, but in another couple of minutes, with the amount of exertion you were putting out, you'd have been dead."

I opened my arms like some cheap magician, the blanket falling to the floor. "Yet here I am."

She shook her head and started off. "Having not learned a thing." Pausing for a moment, she turned. "Mind you, there have been cases up near Seattle, where I was living before. There was a guy who fell off a ferry in British Columbia and was carried thirty miles before they found him near Orcas Island eight hours later. Then there was this woman who fell off a sailboat near the mouth of the Fraser River, and she was out there for seven hours — of course, neither of them were in water as cold as what you were in tonight." She considered me as I mapped the freckles on her nose. "The woman said she made it because there were mermaids in the water keeping her company the whole time. Did you see anything out of the ordinary tonight?"

I picked up my security blanket. "Nope."

She nodded and then turned, heading back into the hospital's inner sanctum, but then stopped to look at me. "Extraordinary, what you did. Extraordinarily stupid or brave, but there's a woman back here who is alive because of your actions."

I threw a thumb at the Cheyenne Nation. "More his."

"Maybe, but he didn't get wet."

I shrugged. "Like a cat, he's smart that way."

She shook her head, her red hair bouncing in rhythm, and then disappeared as Jim turned to us, putting a hand on my shoulder to guide me back into my seat. "What happened out there?"

"She fell."

Thomas sat across from me and stared. "She fell?"

"Yep."

"You want to elaborate or enhance that statement?"

"Not really. She got out of the car and went over to the guardrail to sit on the other side, and the fog was really thick and she slipped."

There was a long pause. "Slipped."

"Yep."

He stared at me a moment more, then, without taking his eyes off me, asked Henry, "She slipped — that your story, too, Bear?"

The Cheyenne Nation's words vibrated against the plate glass. "Yes."

The big trooper eyed me up and down. "You slip, too?"

"No, I'm genuinely stupid and jumped in."

He glanced at Henry and then back to me. "That's your story, huh?"

"Yep."

"We'll see what Rosey says when she gets a little more coherent." He sat in one of the mauve chairs, his hands trailing onto his knees. "So, you heard it?"

Henry turned around. "Yes, we did. We all did."

"Hmm . . . Well, that certainly puts a new timber on things." He sighed, suddenly looking very tired. "I guess we're going to have to start looking for anybody that would have the equipment to break onto our frequency, and it's certainly localized, seeing as how we can't even get it on our radios up here. With a little luck we should be able to triangulate the position of the transmitter and get whoever is doing this. I mean, back in the old days when you just had radio frequency, this stuff would've been hard, but now that we've got this WYOLINK system, the name, unit number, and everything should come up, even a GPS or last event providing the location of the sender."

"None of us were in the car to see the radio or the GPS." I glanced around the room for options, finally coming up with one. "I'm betting you have an expert on radios."

"In Cheyenne, at our centralized dispatch center, we've got a tech person who's a whiz."

"How about to the south, could anyone have heard the radio calls down there? In Shoshoni, Riverton?"

"I don't know, but certainly if someone had heard the repeated calls they would've commented on it, and if it's on our frequency, then it would have to be another HP."

"Would you mind checking with other law enforcement to see if anybody's heard anything? I mean, it would help us confirm where the transmissions are coming from."

"Sure, I'll check around, and I'll have the radio expert give you a call."

I thumbed at the Cheyenne Nation. "Call him — I still don't have a phone."

Thomas yawned. "I will, but I think I'll

do it in the morning."

"A 10-46."

"And what is a 10-46?"

The Bear was driving my truck as I read the official, circa-1979 Wyoming Highway Patrol report from the file that Jim Thomas had given us. "Assisting motorist."

The Cheyenne Nation veered down the Wind River Canyon Scenic Byway, enjoying the way the big V-10 pulled out of the curves. "So, he was assisting a motorist before he pulled out in front of the truck?"

I continued reading. "He cleared the call, and then it was another ten minutes before the accident with the tanker."

"Still, it would be interesting to know who and what it was that close to the event of his death."

"No way to tell — they aren't going to have records that go back that far, especially if it was just a motorist-assistance call." I glanced up at the road and then to him. "Why?"

He shrugged. "I am always interested when someone commits an act such as Womack's as to what their conversation might have been previously."

I grunted. "Probably something along the lines of 'That spare should get you to Far-

124

son, where they have ice cream' or 'I think I've given you enough gas to get you to the Shell station in Shoshoni.' ''

He glanced at the files in my lap. "Anything else?"

"Not really. They're pretty cut and dry and match up with the newspaper articles Rosey found." I closed the file. "Okay, let's go out on a limb here."

"In what direction?"

"Let's pretend that this is Bobby Womack's . . . um, spirit."

"Okay."

"And let's say he didn't take the silver dollars from the bank robbers."

"Yes."

"Then why is he handing them out now?"

The Bear drove for a while in silence. "Perhaps he is attempting to show us that he now knows where the money is."

"Why?"

"To clear his name."

Watching the entrance to the north tunnel approaching, I gestured for the Bear to pull over a little farther than where we'd been parked last night. "Over here, I don't want to have to walk too far."

He slowed and stopped next to the guardrail. "Do you want to get out on my side to avoid going near the water?"

"Very funny."

There was a buzzing noise, and he reached into the inside pocket of his duster. Pulling out his phone, he stared at the screen momentarily before handing it to me. "The Wyoming Highway Patrol Central Dispatch Headquarters in Cheyenne."

I took the thing. "How do you know it's for me?"

"Lucky guess."

I punched the button and stepped out of my truck and sat on the guardrail facing the water just to spite Henry. "Sheriff Walt Longmire."

"Sheriff, this is Eunice Wallace of the Central Dispatch Headquarters in Cheyenne."

"You can't fool me, there's nothing centralized about Cheyenne."

She laughed. "Or organized, for that matter. How can I help you, Sheriff?"

"Jim Thomas says you're the radio guru down there and that you could help us with a problem we're having."

"And that's in Absaroka County?"

I glanced around at the unparalleled beauty of the canyon, looking so different than last night. "I'm actually in the Wind River Canyon even as we speak, and I suppose we're lucky to be speaking, the reception being what it is." I explained the situation, leaving out the more incredible parts and focusing on the possibility of someone illegally breaking in on the Highway Patrol frequency.

"Well, it's possible, but with the trunking systems it would be difficult."

The Cheyenne Nation came around the corner of my truck, I suppose to check to see if I had fallen in the river, and then waved and disappeared. "Here's my first question, what's trunking?"

There was a pause. "Your county has the smallest population in the state, doesn't it?"

"We're small but mighty — why do you ask?"

"Well, you're probably still using a singular frequency?"

"Ever since Marconi sent over that first unit."

"Well, that's a luxury that most departments no longer have. As municipalities and organizations grow, they use more and more radio frequencies for operations, consequently free bandwidth has become more difficult to find."

"Yep, we don't have that problem."

"No, I'd imagine not. Anyway, the radio manufacturers came up with a system that works like a trunk telephone line. Let's use a city like Casper for example — they used to have two or three frequencies for their police department, two or three for the fire department, and then one for public works and one for parks. With the trunking system they have more than fifty user groups on ten radio frequencies."

"How can you do that?"

"One of the frequencies is the control or data channel that continually broadcasts a computer data stream that sounds like a chainsaw on the air."

I thought about the noise that Rosey had said preceded the mysterious radio calls. "A chainsaw, huh?"

"Something like that. But to get back to your question, every time an officer or firefighter or anybody presses their microphone button, a simultaneous computer command is sent out to everyone in that person's radio group and moves them to one of the nine other available frequencies within the system."

"Sounds complicated."

"It is — the channel assignments are completely random, so there's no way to monitor communications unless you have a computer-assisted trunk-tracker system."

"So, where could you get something like that?"

"Best Buy or Radio Shack, if they were still in business."

I removed the phone from my ear to enable a full-force face palm of epic proportions and then returned it. "You're kidding."

" 'Fraid not — any 800 megahertz scanner with a microphone would work as long as it's calibrated properly." She waited a moment, probably sensing my dissatisfaction with that bit of information. "Trunking systems are pretty hard to program for the uninitiated, so you're probably looking for someone who has a knowledge of radios and computers."

"What's the range on those types of scanners?"

"Well, you see, the transmission would depend on elevation, obstructions, transmitter power. . . ."

I glanced up at the two-thousand-foot walls. "We're in the canyon."

"Ten to twenty miles at best." There was a longer pause. "Where are you right now?"

"Preparing to throw myself in the Wind River."

She laughed. "Are you near the tunnels?"

I stood, stepped back over the guardrail, and looked across the hood of my truck, where I could see the Bear standing by the entrance of the northernmost borehole.

"North entrance."

"Look up." I did as she told me and spotted a thin structure passing between the clouds, periodically giving off a glowing red light, like a pulse. "That tower is only about a decade old. When the old-timers used to head into the canyon they'd call it in and that was the last you heard of them until they came out on the other end — they used to call it No-Man's-Land."

9

"No-Man's-Land, huh?"

I nodded, but it was difficult with the 240-pound man sitting on my shoulders. "The first time the term was used was back in 1320, *nonesmanneslond,* which was used to describe disputed territory between two kingdoms; then it was the name for a place outside the walls of London that was used for executions and even a spot on the forecastle of ships."

"Um-hmm."

I shifted the Cheyenne Nation's weight a little. "Of course, the term that's used today is a result of the trench warfare in World War I."

"Of course."

"Or the cold war, concerning the iron curtain." I shifted his and my weight again, trying to ease the pressure on my stoved-up leg.

"Would you stop fidgeting?"

I steadied myself on the makeshift side-walk, which was barely wide enough for me, let alone the both of us. "I'm just trying to get comfortable, which isn't easy. It's not like you're a lightweight."

"Look who is talking."

A few pieces of rock and debris fell past my face. "What, exactly, are you doing up there?"

"There are patched spots of concrete here and along the ceilings of all the tunnels."

"So?"

"Some look newer than others."

"So?" There was a jolt and more dust and tiny pieces of concrete fell, one bouncing off my head. "Ouch."

"Ah, there are bolts driven into the ceiling, I am assuming to stabilize the roof."

"Can I put you down now?" Without waiting for a response, I checked both ways and then stepped off the curb backward, leaning forward and allowing Henry to step off onto the sidewalk. "So?"

He turned and looked down the tunnels, the sunlight intermittently shining in the openings between. "The two robbers worked for WYDOT. If you were going to hide something in these tunnels, where would you hide it?"

"I see your point." I studied the ceiling

and walls. "There's only one problem — there must be a couple hundred patch spots just in this tunnel alone." I looked at him. "There's another problem with your theory. If I was on the lam, and the cops were closing in, I'm not sure how much time I'd have for masonry work."

"What would you have done?"

"I would've chucked the bag over the guardrail or into the water and hoped I could come back for it later."

He thought about it. "Where, exactly, did the shootout take place?"

"About a quarter mile up the road around the next bend."

"So, Womack was waiting for them as part of a roadblock."

"I guess. It's in the folder in my truck."

"Why not stop them in the tunnel, where they are contained?"

I smiled. "You're thinking like a soldier instead of a cop. In these situations, you always have to allow for the citizenry. What happens if you stop them in the tunnel and a vacationing family pulls up behind them?"

He nodded. "End of vacation."

As we walked back to the Bullet, I voiced something that had been on my mind since the conversation with the woman from the Highway Patrol's central office. "The dispatcher in Cheyenne said that they used to call the canyon No-Man's-Land, because they couldn't get radio reception in here until they put in that new tower on the top of the wall." I pointed to the structure. "That thing went in ten-odd years ago, and that's long after Bobby Womack's demise."

"Yes."

"It's highly unlikely that you could get any reception on the spot where he chose to intercept them."

"That is true."

I glanced back at the dark opening. "And there would've been no reception in those tunnels, but there damn well would've been on the other side at the Boysen Reservoir."

"So, you are coming around to my questioning the location of contact?"

"Maybe, but I'm more concerned with where he was when he heard about the APB on the bank robbers, because he couldn't have been in the canyon. Then there's the motorist-assistance call just before the tanker incident in which he lost his life and the incident itself."

"He could not have been in the canyon when he received these calls."

"That's correct." We arrived at my truck, and I looked up the road. "But especially the one that cost him his life. If he didn't receive any radio call about the runaway truck . . ." I pointed north to the far end of the S-curve that disappeared around the rock cliffs. "The first time he would've seen it would've been when it came around that turn, up where he shot those two men."

"Coincidence?"

"I don't know, but I sure would like to know what he was thinking." I pulled the door open on my truck and climbed in as the Bear did the same on the other side. "Any ideas?"

"Your primary interest seems to be in discovering the truth about what might have happened with the robbery and the death of Bobby Womack."

I fired up the Bullet and slipped her in gear. "I'm always more interested in the truth, no matter what the subject."

He pointed south. "Then we should go to Fort Washakie and find the missing aunt of Bobby Womack."

Finding somebody on the rez can be a tricky business, but nothing Henry Standing Bear couldn't handle, at least that's what I thought. Henry called Kimama, but she wasn't home — I suggested she was probably out riding her broom.

We stopped at the Catholic church to ask

a redheaded priest from New England where we might find Bobby Womack's aunt, and he told us to talk to the bartender at the Rezeride down the road. The bartender knew a guy over in Fort Washakie who knew another fellow who had gone to school with a Womack; he wasn't sure of the number but gave us an address. The woman at the address had lived in the house for only three years, but she said that the previous owners had been elderly and that the husband had died and the woman had sold her the house and moved to Fort Washakie proper. We checked the city hall, and they had a listing for a Theona Womack, but when we drove up, the house had burned down. We knocked on the doors of a few neighbors and got varying stories, some saying the old woman had moved, some of the versions saying as far as Canada.

We finally gave up and headed north, coming to rest at the Cee Nokuu Café at the Wind River Casino, where we filled our stomachs with Indian tacos and iced tea. "She's probably dead."

The Cheyenne Nation shrugged, taking the last sip of his tea and standing. "I have one more secret weapon that I am about to employ. Stay here."

"Okay." I finished my meal and waited,

getting a free refill from the machine and sitting back down in time for Henry to reenter. "She is in the next room."

"Who?"

"Theona Womack." He gestured to the wall to our left. "They have Blue-Hair-Charity-Slots for Tots in the event room on Thursday mornings here at the casino. They are almost done, but I will warn you that she is not alone."

"How are you, Bucket?"

"I'm fine, you old bat, how are you?" She snickered, and I was starting to get a feel for how you dealt with Kimama Bellefeuille. Pulling a chair out for Theona, I was careful pushing it back in, afraid I would break the seemingly mummified woman if I wasn't careful. Theona made Kimama look like a spring chicken.

The Bear sat beside her, holding her hand and speaking low in Arapaho, which left me out of the equation. I turned and looked at Kimama as she sipped a Dr Pepper from a can with a straw. "How much did you win?"

She flapped a hand in dismissal. "I lost seventeen dollars."

"I thought you could see the future?"

"I can, and I saw myself losing eighteen dollars, so I made out all right. Besides, it's

137

all for charity." She sipped her soda some more, and her dark eyes glistened. "I heard the flat-hat went swimming."

"She did."

"I heard you did, too."

"Yep."

"Did it cool you off?"

"Yep."

"Did he try and warm you back up?"

I stared at her. "What?"

"Heeci'ecihit, when you met him, did he try to warm you?"

I thought about the delusions I'd had last night, having convinced myself that that was what they were. "What are you talking about?"

Without a moment of hesitation, she reached an arthritic finger out and tapped the coin in my shirt pocket with a fingertip that felt like wood. "You saw him."

I was astonished that not only did she know I had the coin, but she knew exactly where it was. I stumbled for a response. "I . . . I'm not sure what I saw."

She nodded her head and smiled at the surface of the table. "You are not the first to see him, Bucket."

"Have you seen him?"

She ignored me and began listening to the conversation going on at the other side of the table. After a while she readjusted herself on her chair and looked out toward the center of the casino, where all the amputee bandits clanged and beeped, clamoring for attention. "The machines, they don't take quarters like they used to, very dissatisfying for those of us who like the noise." She turned back to look at me. "My husband and I were coming back from a sweat one summer some years ago, headed for Thermopolis, when we overheated in the canyon. We were just sitting there waiting for the automobile to cool itself when one of the flat-hats pulled in behind us. We had been having an argument, and we'd been drinking a little. The flat-hat came up and asked my husband for his license. He kept shining his flashlight in on us, making it hard to see him, but his voice sounded strange and familiar."

I glanced over and could see Henry and Theona watching Kimama as she told the story.

"He stood there with my husband's license for a long time, but then he handed it back to him and told him that his license only had a year left on it. My husband was glad to get it back without having to do anything else and assured the flat-hat that he would get another one in a year." She sipped her soda. "I'll never forget what the flat-hat said next."

Duly prompted, I asked, "What did he say?"

"He said he wouldn't have to." She sat the can back on the table. "Eleven months later my husband died." A long moment passed as Henry and Theona regrouped their conversation, and then Kimama spoke again in a low voice. "You know how he died?"

"Your husband?"

She made a long, exasperated noise through her clenched teeth. "No, Heeci'ecihit, the Highwayman."

"Well . . ."

Her head slipped to the side, and she eyed me at an angle. "He died in fire. It is a bad way to go."

"I don't know if there are any good ones."

She flapped the hand at me again. "There are many, but fire is bad. The terrible thing about fire is that you become one with the wind, your ashes carried around the world over and over again seeking peace but finding none. Every time Heeci'ecihit attempts to come to rest, the winds pick him up, blowing on the embers of his soul and carrying him further."

I cleared my throat and leaned in. "So, if we were so inclined, how could we find peace for him?"

I sat there looking at her, and the noises from the casino seemed to fade away and we might've been sitting in the canyon with only the sound of the water and the wind around us. "The dead only want the same as the living."

"Which is?"

"To be understood, but to help him be understood you must first understand him." She studied me for a long time. "I have decided to help you."

"In what way?"

"I think it is time we did a purification ceremony in the canyon and do what we can to help Heeci'ecihit find the peace he deserves."

"You don't think he stole the money?"

"No. I do not, but there are those who do. I would say that is part of what keeps him restless and riding the wind."

"What else?"

"Things I cannot say — things you will have to discover on your own."

She glanced at Theona and lowered her voice. "The family has had a hard life, harder since Bobby died, but she did not know him that well."

"And you did?"

Her eyes came up sharp. "Yes, I did."

It was a hunch, but that's how I make my living, so I did something I tried never to do. "Kimama, how old are you?"

The darts in her eyes faded, and she smiled. "I do not know."

Her tone was coy, but I was pretty sure. "Don't know, or won't tell me?"

"How old do you think I am, Bucket?"

"I'm guessing, mind you, but there's one known fact that gives me an idea." I leaned forward, placing an elbow on the table and crowding her personal space, but she didn't even bat an eye. "Bobby Womack was thirty-two years old when he died and if you're about the same age as he was and Sam Little Soldier, which I think you are, then that would put you somewhere around seventy." I waited a few seconds and then added, "I bet I'm close."

She rested her hands on her lap and stared at the floor. "Thirty-two does not sound so old now, does it?"

"Sometimes it's as old as you get."

She pulled at her lip as if stretching it might loosen the words. "My marriage was a bad marriage to begin with and when I discovered I could not have children, it got worse. My husband held it against me — he was a big man and struck me often. He would not grant me a divorce. It is strange, but in those days such a thing was unheard of. Bobby and me started seeing each other on the sly. Nobody knew about it, but I would often drive up into the canyon to be with him."

"Did he ever say anything about the men he'd shot?"

"Yes, he talked of it many times. It was a great sorrow to him that he had to do such a thing and especially to two of his own people. He said he had no choice, that they had pointed their guns at him and he had responded the way he had been trained, and now they were dead."

I pulled the coin from my pocket and handed it to her. "The flat-hat, Rosey, has been finding one of these just before something terrible happens in the canyon."

She felt the silver dollar in her hand, running her thumb over the surface but not looking at it. "You received this one?"

"Yep."

"When?"

"Last night, in the tunnels."

"Did something terrible happen?"

I thought about it as I watched her fingers run over the coin and then decided an attempted suicide pretty much fit the bill. "Yep, I guess you could say that."

"But the flat-hat, she lives?"

"Yep."

"Because of you."

"I suppose, and Henry." I brought my eyes up to her. "Did he ever say anything about the money?"

"No, but people talked because he was Indian." She looked out at the casino again. "Things have changed but maybe not so much."

"Did it bother him, the things that people said?"

Her eyes turned back, and she studied me. "Would they have bothered you, those words?"

I pulled at the corners of my mouth with a thumb and forefinger. "Did they bother him enough that he might've killed himself?" She started to speak, but I cut her off. "I've seen where he died, Kimama. There was no way he could've gotten a radio call in the no-man's-land of the canyon warning him about the tanker. From where he sat at the north tunnel he would've had thirty seconds or so to make up his mind to pull out in front of that thing . . ."

She broke into my monologue. "He didn't kill himself."

"How can you be so sure?"

She leaned in close, and I could feel the

warmth of her breath. "Because, Bucket, I was there."

10

"Does Jim Thomas know you're on duty?"

"I'm fine."

"Seeing as how you drowned last night? You were in that water longer than I was, and I don't feel so great myself." I leaned on the Dodge and continued scolding her through the window as she clutched her forehead and we watched the tiny flakes descend like a gently disturbed snow globe. "Headache?"

She nodded. "Just a little."

"You need to go home. Now."

"I want to be here for the ceremony. It's important."

I sighed and looked at the promontory at the end of the pull-off that overlooked the Wind River, where Henry was conferring with Kimama and Sam Little Soldier. "It's just a ceremony — nothing says it's going to work."

She dropped her hand and looked up at

me with the icy blue eyes. "You still don't believe any of this, do you?"

"Nope."

"Even after hearing it?"

I laid an arm on the roof of her car, leaning in and smiling. "It's a radio, Rosey, somebody's on the other end, and it's not Bobby Womack."

"How can you be so sure?"

"A feeling."

"A feeling?"

"Yep." I glanced around for effect. "Look, I've seen some amazing things in this life, some things I can't explain, but I'm not willing to go with the out-of-this-world supposition until it's been proven to me that it's not of this world. That's part of our job, to find answers, and I'm not willing to throw up my hands and say there are none until I'm sure there aren't any." She said nothing, so I continued. "Someone is making those radio calls, and someone is putting those silver dollars on the road." I pulled the one from my pocket and handed it to her.

The blue ice in her eyes melted, and the whites glistened in the dim light of the cruiser. "Where did you get this?"

I glanced over my right shoulder back down the road. "North entrance of the north tunnel."

"How?"

"When I took that walk through the tunnels, I heard footsteps behind me and chased after them."

"Who was it?"

"I didn't see, but they left that coin on the road for me."

"Did anything bad happen, because if it didn't, it's going to. I told you about the other times when —"

"You tried to kill yourself."

"What?"

"You attempted to kill yourself — I'd say that's pretty bad."

She looked away. "I don't remember."

"Jumping?"

"No."

"Well, you really didn't jump, you just stepped off."

Her hand came up, and she grabbed the zipper of my jacket. "I don't remember any of it, Walt. Nothing. I just remember laying beside this unit and hearing that voice, repeating over and over and over."

"Well, you missed the exciting part."

She continued studying the silver dollar. "This one is different, marked up." She looked at me. "Did anything else happen? I mean anything bad?"

I thought about it. "I almost got run over by not paying attention." I reached out and tapped the coin in her hand. "Slipped on this thing and then found it, that's why it's scratched."

"Hold on, that was before we waited for the call and before you talked to me?"

"Yep."

She pushed open the door and then slammed it, careful to pull the tail of her black slicker aside. She stared at me as she held the silver dollar up between us. "You had this on you and didn't say anything?"

"I wanted to wait until we did or didn't hear the radio call."

"If we hadn't heard anything would you have shown me this?"

"Of course."

"Then why did you wait?"

"Because I didn't want to confuse the issue."

"Which is?"

"Whether or not you were actually hearing the radio calls."

She held the coin closer to my face. "This is proof."

I stood there for a moment and then took the thing from her, holding it up into the ghostly pall of the half-hidden moon. "No. This is an 1888 Hot Lips Morgan silver dollar — and that's all it is. You can buy one in mint condition in any coin shop in the country for about three hundred and fifty dollars and that's what somebody has done." I glanced at the winding roadway beside us. "And then they've placed them on this road for you and me to find." I looked back at her. "We have a very clear objective here, Rosey, and that's finding out who is doing this and why — and that, not all the burning of incense, chanting, and magic words in the world, is going to accomplish it."

"Just another day on the job, huh?"

I nodded, returned the coin to my pocket, and glanced around at the two-thousand-foot cliffs. My eyes were drawn to the thick belt of the Milky Way galaxy and the dense stream of stars that ran from one end of the canyon to the other, still visible even with the falling flurries — the Hanging Road, as the Cheyenne and Crow called it, the path the owls used to take messages back and forth between the land of the living and the Camp of the Dead.

"You're wrong about one thing, though."

I looked down at her. "What's that?"

She glanced at the road, but then her attention turned south, toward the northern entrance of the north tunnel. "The silver dollars may be warnings of impending disasters, but we have the power to avert them."

"Excuse me?"

"At least you do. You could've been hit by the car, but the coin saved you, and I could've drowned, but you saved me. So that means that the silver dollars and therefore the highwayman don't have absolute sway."

I thought about it. "Yep, but then again if this dollar saved me and I saved you, then maybe they do." Draping an arm over her shoulders, I turned her around, steering her toward the Indian ceremony. "C'mon, let's go listen to some chanting and magical words."

She reached up and gripped my arm as we approached the promontory that stretched out past the guardrail. "Will there be incense?" Her voice carried a false enthusiasm. "You said there would be incense."

I sighed. "There's always incense, cedar, or sage. You want to put money on it?"

"I'll bet you a dollar."

I laughed and hugged her in a little. "I bet you will."

"Nenéé-' ne-nihiióó." Kimama raised her

arms and looked out over the roiling water of the Wind River, raising her face to the gentle snowflakes and crying out in a strange rhythm that was at once startling and melodic. "Tei'yoonóh'-o' hootn-I'-iiióó-i'."

There wasn't much room out on the point where she'd decided to have the ceremony because of the small fire, so the rest of us were relegated to watching her from behind. Sam Little Soldier was the closest, along with Henry, who stood holding the ubiquitous pottery bowl, the sweet-grass bundles, and the juniper or big cedar, a third in a duel with ghosts.

"Noh heetéetoo-no."

The Bear had discussed the ceremony with me, explaining that it wasn't an exorcism but more of a plea that the spirit should find peace in this world and finally be allowed to proceed to the next. "Noncombative" was the way the Cheyenne Nation had described it. He had laughed at this point and posited the thought that trying to get the spirits of the departed to do what we wanted was a low-sum game in that they had lost everything, and what in the world did we have to offer in exchange?

"Ci'céésé nenéé-né-nihiioo."

I'd repeated the quote from Kimama about the dead wanting only what the living wanted — understanding. He'd made a face and asked if all I really wanted in life was to be understood, and I'd told him that a comfortable pair of boots was nice.

"Niicííhoh-o nonohkú-nihiit-ówoo."

"I'm glad there's incense."

I glanced down at Rosey and was happy to see that some of her old energy had returned. "I'm glad the AIRFA was passed, or we would all have been arrested."

Leaning into me, she whispered. "The what?"

"American Indian Religious Freedom Act — it was established to allow the Native peoples the right to preserve their religious and cultural practices. It allows them access to sacred sites and the freedom to worship through ceremony with possession of objects considered sacred."

"Hihcébe niiéi'-noh'eeséihi-n biikóó."

"Ancient history."

"1978."

"You're kidding."

"Nope. Talk about an infringement on your religious freedoms, huh?"

"Cih-tokoohob-éi'ee."

Rosey focused on the woman presiding over the ceremony. "She looks familiar to me."

"You stop her?"

She took a moment. "I don't think so, but maybe that's it."

"Cih-'ówouunon-in."

"Kimama had some interesting things to say this afternoon; evidently, she was with Bobby Womack the evening he was killed."

Rosey turned to look at me. "Really?"

"She was having an affair with him."

"Bobby wasn't married."

"No, but she was."

"Cese'éihii técénéniihenéihii niihii-een."

"She would drive up into the canyon at night to spend time with him in some crappy station wagon she drove." I noticed a peculiar look on Rosey's face. "Those were her words. Something wrong?"

Her brow twisted. She saw me studying her and laughed lightly. "It's nothing. I'm just getting sentimental about my mother lately. "My father died a number of years ago, but my mother's health is starting to fail."

"Nookóox noh neixóó! Cih-eeh'étii-'!"

"She nearby?"

"Not really. She's in Cheyenne — she's in a home. Don't get me wrong, it's a nice place, but I don't get enough opportunities to get there and visit her the way I should. I'd move her, but she's been there for seven years and I don't want to upset her by taking her to a new place."

"Heeyoocéi'oo-' hoowuóów."

"It's difficult."

"Yeah."

We watched as Henry passed the bowl, the sweet-grass braids, and the big cedar to Kimama, and she lowered the offerings into the small fire, catching the ends and allowing them to burn before twisting them partially out in the pottery. She held the bowl in her left hand, scooping the wisps of smoke like captured spirits and rolling them over her head and arms; then she switched the bowl to her other hand and repeated the procedure. "Beneesooo-' hiine'etiit, henihihc-owooyeitieenee."

I stepped a little away from the others, and my eyes played to the right. I half turned toward the road in order to look back at the opening of the northernmost tunnel. Shadow had engulfed the wall of granite that scooped out and faced north, but I could still make out the utter darkness of the tunnel itself.

It was like an opening to another place, and I guess I half expected to see the ghostly apparition of Bobby Womack looking back at me from the abyss. I didn't see him, and if Kimama and her magic words that floated up to meet the flurries had their way, I never would.

I was a little sad, because as people go, Bobby Womack had never done anyone real harm — his spirit had warned of disaster but had never caused it. If the stories of the canyon were true, he'd helped people all these years and never harmed a soul. If there was a kernel of possibility in all this, where was it I would be spending eternity? Guarding the denizens of Absaroka County — a ghost sheriff?

"Heetih-nohkú-ni'-cebísee-t heet-íeti-'."

They were wrapping up the ceremony, and I pulled out my pocket watch to check the time — it was eleven o'clock. Rosey and I strolled back toward the parked vehicles and stopped at her cruiser as the group at large approached. Henry and Sam assisted Kimama as she stepped over the guardrail but then released her as she dismissed the two of them with a wave of both hands.

Rosey was leaning in the open door of her vehicle, I'm sure aware of the time.

Kimama moved toward Sam's car but stopped a little away from it to berate me. "You talked too much during the ceremony, Bucket."

I was unaware that she could hear me but apologetic just the same. "Sorry."

"You should have respect."

"I do, and I'm sorry." I gestured toward Rosey. "We just had a few things we needed to discuss."

She glanced at the trooper and then back to me. "Next time, do not do it while I am working."

"Yes, ma'am."

She started to walk past Rosey but took a moment to reach out and grip her arm. "And you, Hookuuhulu', you should know better." She looked straight at her for another moment and then continued on as Rosey watched after her.

She looked back at me with a quizzical expression mixed with shock. "What did she just call me?"

"It sounded like *Hookuuhulu'*?"

"Little mouse." We both turned to see Sam Little Soldier stepping up beside us with Henry. "Hookuuhulu,' it is Arapaho for 'Little Mouse,' an endearment that everyone uses for children and grand-children."

Rosey swallowed and shook her head, looking back at the woman as she climbed in Sam's ancient Toyopet Crown. "My mother, she said there was a nanny who used to call me 'Little Mouse.' "

"Maybe she was Arapaho." Sam Little

Soldier passed us and continued toward the vintage Toyota, probably afraid the medicine woman would hot-wire it. "But in case you haven't noticed, Kimama has a nickname for everyone."

"I noticed." I moved up beside Rosey as the Bear joined us. "Speaking of, where's Joey these days?"

"He's not a big one for ceremonies."

I pointed toward Kimama. "I don't suppose she's got a nickname herself?"

He opened the driver's-side door and spoke, just before wedging inside to escape the falling snow, "Nope, just 'Kimama.' "

As he started the rattletrap of a car and shuddered his way past us in a loop toward the road with his window down, I yelled, "And what does that mean?"

He turned his head toward the sha-woman as she stuffed things into her oversized purse and then stuck his big head out the window one last time to shout at us as they drove by leaving melted tracks in the gravel. "It's Shoshone — it means Butterfly."

11

"So, Kimama was Butterfly, your nanny."

"I . . . I guess so."

"Are you okay?"

She leaned against her car and crossed her arms, the snow collecting on her slicker and then quickly melting. "Yeah, just a little shaken, I guess." She was silent for a while. "It was like hearing a voice from your past, you know?"

"I would imagine."

She drew in a deep breath and looked up at me, her eyes fogged with tears. "I need to talk with her."

"I bet."

"No, I mean now."

I glanced at Henry, sitting on the Dodge's grill guard with his back to us as though he weren't paying any attention. "Well, we can cover your duty while you go run her down. It won't take very long to catch that beater."

She glanced around, unsure of herself but

finally making a decision. "No, I need to stay here in the canyon. Can you go and get her? Bring her back so I can talk to her?"

It seemed like a strange streak of logic. "Tonight?"

"Now. I need to talk to her now. Please?"

"Okay." I glanced at Henry, who had turned and was looking at us from over one shoulder. "Let's go."

We piled into my truck and drove north in the direction that the Toyopet Crown had headed, the flurries seeming serious all of a sudden, and I hoped this was not going to turn into one of those spring blizzards. I wondered why Rosey had insisted on staying in the canyon but figured she wanted to in case the radio transmission came through again.

"Why do you suppose she wants to stay there?"

"I am not sure — maybe she is expecting another radio call?"

I flipped on my windshield wipers. "But why does she care at this point? We heard it, so she knows it's not a ghost — so why does she feel compelled to stay there?" I thought back about something I'd heard, something someone had said. "There was something Jim Thomas said about Mike Harlow — that he made mention that no

160

one ever really got out of the canyon, so why not stay?"

"Perhaps Rosey has fallen prey to the same psychosis."

"You think there's a geographically specific psychosis?"

He glanced up at the towering granite walls. "It is a unique place, and it is possible that people are responding to it in a particular way."

Hustling through the curves, I spotted lights up ahead. "Wouldn't be the first time."

There were a pair of dim headlights, but the vehicle looked too large to be the Toyota and, with its lights pointed toward us, it was going the wrong way. As we slowed, I could see that it was the Coleman oil tanker, the driver probably pulling over to cool his brakes.

The outlaw was out of his truck and was kicking something underneath the tanker, maybe trying to eke out another couple of miles from the old Diamond Rio.

Figuring he wasn't my problem at the moment, I accelerated through the turn and could see the taillights of the vintage car heading around the next curve. I hit the gas and caught up with Sam in the next straight-away. Switching on the emergencies, I blipped my siren and pulled them over near the rock wall between the reflector posts.

Jumping out, I slammed the door behind me and moved through the eighth of an inch of slush that was trying to decide if it was going to turn to ice or melt. I got up to the driver's side and tapped on the window. Sam cranked it down and looked at me. "Rosey wants to talk to Kimama."

"What about?"

I leaned down to look across at her. "She thinks you might've been her nanny when she was young."

Lowering herself over the center console, she squinted at me. "Bucket, have you been drinking?"

"When she was a child, she lived here — well, down in Riverton — and she told me that she had a nanny who was called Butterfly, who used to call her Little Mouse. Does any of that sound familiar to you?"

Her eyes widened, and her hand came up to cover her gaping mouth as she leaned across the car to look at me closer. "The flat-hat, she was a child here?"

"Yep."

"When?"

"I'm not sure — thirty-five years ago?"

Her hand fumbled across Sam as he reached out and steadied her. "Kimama,

162

are you all right?"

"The flat-hat, where is she?"

I nodded due south. "Back at the tunnel. Why?"

"I must go to her."

I stepped back. "C'mon, you can ride with me."

Sam held fast. "No, I will bring her. You go ahead, and we will follow."

"Okay." I started to go but then turned and pointed a finger at both of them and spoke in my authoritative voice. "Hey, put on your seat belts." I carefully jogged back to the Bullet, where Henry was waiting. Closing the door, I started the ten cylinders and turned back south. "Why'd you stay in the truck?"

"Because I could not get out — you lodged it against the cliff." He looked at the old Toyota. "What did Kimama say?"

"She knows her. Has to — it's too much of a coincidence. The names, the timing, and she said she needed to see her immediately."

"The same thing Rosey said."

I turned on my emergency lights. "Yep."

"Thirty-six years."

"Kimama said thirty-five but close enough."

"That would have been approximately

when Bobby Womack died."

I thought about it as I swerved to miss the slow-moving tanker that Coleman had gotten back on the road, then watched as he steered into the pullout behind me and ground to a stop, probably in an attempt to avoid any more brushes with the law. "Yep."

The Bear turned to look at me in the dim light of the cab, the greenish glow of the instrument panel reflecting off the sharp angles of his face. "What has changed in the canyon?"

I flipped off the emergency lights. "What?"

"The conversation we had previously about what could have been the catalyst for all this."

I thought about the conclusion we'd drawn, the one that hadn't seemed to make sense at the time. "Rosey."

He turned toward the Wind River. "Rosey." His voice resounded against the closed window, his breath fogging the surface. "She was there, too."

More than a few hairs stood up on the back of my neck. "The night Bobby Womack was killed."

He turned to look at me. "Yes."

"She was with Kimama?"

"Kimama said that she used to come up into the canyon to visit him while they were

164

having their affair, and if she was babysitting for Rosey she must have brought her with her."

I sputtered. "Okay, let's say she was there. What in the world, or out of it for that matter, would've started these radio communications after all these years?"

He raised his hands and gestured at the cliffs. "Rosey returning to the canyon."

I shook my head and laughed. "Henry . . ."

"She became what he was, a trooper. Someone made the connection between the two. Bobby never had children, suppose he made some kind of spiritual link with Rosey. Her return could have triggered all of this."

"Just so you know, you are way out on a limb with this hypothesis."

He braced a hand on the dash as we made the last turn. "Do you have another?"

I put my foot on the brakes and slowed, feeling the rear of the three-quarter-ton break traction before pulling into the service area in front of the north tunnel. "Not yet, but I will."

I'd barely gotten stopped before Rosey was at my window, the heat of her breath fogging the glass the way Henry's had. "Did you find her?"

"We did — they're coming along behind us." She looked back up the road, but they had yet to appear. "Look, Rosey, I wouldn't get my hopes pinned on all this. It's just a coincidence."

She kept looking north. "It's not." Her eyes turned to me, and the blue there was otherworldly. "I'm remembering things."

Sam Little Soldier joined us at the truck with the spring snow collecting on him as it would on a mountain, and we watched the two women from a distance as they stood by his vintage import and talked. "This gladdens my heart."

"You knew."

He turned to look at Henry and nodded. "About the relationship, yes."

"But not about Rosey's connection with it?"

"No. That was not something Kimama mentioned. I had had my suspicions about her and Bobby, but she had never said anything, and neither did he."

"Then who did?"

He glanced down at the snow, the slush soaking his moccasins. "I would rather not say."

I went ahead and threw in my two cents' worth. "I'd rather you did. All things considered, I don't give a hoot in hell for who's involved with whom, but when it starts having an effect on the performance of a Wyoming trooper and a friend of mine, I want answers."

Sam stepped away from us and turned, his hands still in his pants pockets. "This is not a criminal case."

"No, it's personal." I waited a moment before continuing. "I can find out from Kimama, but I'd rather spare her that."

He stared at me a good long while in the glow of the revolving emergency lights on Rosey's cruiser, glistening yellow from the reflection of the granite canyon walls. "Mike Harlow."

"The trooper?"

"Bobby Womack was his training officer and in that time, he became . . . umm, aware of the situation."

Henry and I looked at each other as I turned back to Sam. "And he kept his mouth shut?"

"The thin blue line." Sam smiled. "And they were friends."

"Did Harlow make the connection between Rosey and the little girl that used to accompany Kimama?"

"I doubt it — none of the rest of us did." He shrugged. "Besides, all you blond-haired blue eyes look alike to us." His eyes came back up to mine. "And it was thirty-five years ago, man — she was a toddler."

"But . . ." I glanced at the Bear. "Just for argument's sake, why would Womack's soul bond with that little girl anyway?"

Henry took a few steps toward the two women and then turned, his voice carrying back to us. "Kindred spirits."

"There has to be more." They both looked at me. "That night, the night that Bobby died, something happened. Something with the money . . . I don't know." I pointed a finger toward the women. "But at least one of them does."

We watched as the two women finished their conversation and then hugged, long and hard. They stood there holding each other and maybe it was me, but the tall trooper in her long slicker and the tiny medicine woman seemed to change places, and I could almost see them as they had been all those years ago, the sha-woman and the little blond girl who must've loved her more than life itself and gone everywhere with her. It was strange the paths the human heart chose to take and the attachments it made along the way. The surest sign of the altruistic nature of the organ is its ability to ignore race, color, creed, and gender and just blindly love with all its might — one of the most irrefutable forces on earth.

They broke apart, arms still entwined, as they held each other at arm's length, a miracle of synchronicity.

Rosey placed an arm over Kimama's shoulder, and they walked toward us but stopped where Sam's Toyopet Crown sat waiting. They looked at each other again, hugged once more, and then Rosey helped Kimama into her seat, giving Sam a quick look as she closed the door.

"Gotta go." He swung away from us, and he and Rosey exchanged a few words over the metallic blue top of the vehicle before he wedged inside and began cranking on the starter.

Rosey walked toward us as the ancient Toyota finally caught and belched a cloud of bluish black smoke before dying. Sam cranked the starter again, and the Toyota started on the fourth try, rattling to life, stuttering and pulling out, only to die one more time.

Rosey looked back, shaking her head. "I think we may have to push that thing to get it going."

"Maybe."

She slapped the snow from her hat as she cracked open the door of her unit while Henry and I stood by, me pulling my pocket watch from my jeans and reading the time to her. "It's 12:32, in case you were wondering."

She settled in the seat, still watching the Toyota as Sam ground the starter. "You know what? I really don't care."

I smiled down at her. "I'm glad to hear it."

"I can't help but think that it's all over, you know? That Kimama and I were meant to find each other and now that we have, that it's done."

"Maybe so."

Pulling his duster closed and folding his arms, Henry leaned a hip against her car. "Perhaps that is what this was all about."

I continued to smile, but something caught the corner of my eye as I glanced at the road heading north, something shiny. I turned my head, but it still glistened, a sparkle in the snow-dusted road.

Stepping off, I walked toward it down the scenic byway, passing the Toyota as it finally caught and started again. It was up the road, but even in the falling snow it caught the light like a beacon.

Rosey's voice called out after me. "Walt? What are you doing?"

Hoping against hope that it wasn't what I thought it was, I kept walking with my back to them and then stopped. I thought about kicking it to the side of the road and pretending that it wasn't really there, but that's not how the fates work; they align themselves like gears in a giant and inevitable machine, the spanner kicks forward, and the teeth mesh in an inexorable whir, a noise that decides your fate like a roulette wheel.

Walking to the centerline, I turned and knelt, picking up the silver dollar. There were only a few flakes on it and it was warm, very warm. Carefully palming the pocket watch I still held in my right hand, I turned the face upward and read the time.

12:34.

Automatically and in that slow motion that overtakes you in those lean moments of disaster, my eyes went to the tunnel, but no apparition was there, only the sputtering Toyopet Crown, which had shuddered and died once again, stalling just in front of the entrance of the tunnel and coasting to a stop.

As Sam Little Soldier tried the starter again, I turned back to Rosey and Henry, the trooper sitting in the driver's seat of the Dodge with the Bear standing by the door, both of them looking at me. As I stared past the coin, it became more obvious that they were not looking at me but farther up the road.

The whir of foregone conclusion was like a meshing of time and place as I pivoted to my right in time to see the Coleman Heating Oil truck, only a quarter mile away, careen against the guardrail with sparks flying, as the driver overcorrected and bounced off the stone wall on the opposite side of the road. Trailing a rooster tail of sparks, the decrepit tanker shot forward unimpaired, the grimy yellow headlights of the runaway splitting the distance between me and the stalled car at the mouth of the tunnel.

Pushing off the ground at the center of the road, I felt my boots slipping on the snowy surface as I fought to gain traction with the tanker bearing down on me. It slammed into the cliff as Coleman attempted in vain to rub some of the speed off. His arms flailed at the wheel, but it was useless as the big Diamond Rio gained momentum, the side of the truck scraping the rocks again, the sparks arcing and leaping from the metal surface like live cables on an electric streetcar.

I heaved myself to the side of the road and rolled out of the way against the guardrail. The truck thundered by as my eyes caught

the Toyota still attempting to get started —
but, more important, the steadfast and
almost peaceful look on Trooper Wayman's
face as she lifted a leather-gloved hand with
a loose pearl snap and pulled the transmission selector of the black Charger into drive.

Henry's words echoed in my mind.

Kindred spirits.

12

Gripping the guardrail, I pulled myself up and ran toward the tunnel as the Dodge shot forward. Spraying a rooster tail of gravel, snow, and dirt, the vehicle skidded but still stayed on a path that would converge headlong with the runaway tanker.

Henry was also vaulting toward the point of impact, both of us laboring under the delusion that if we could only get there first we might somehow dissuade the tons of steel from their impending impact.

I had the briefest of hopes that Rosey might hit the Diamond Rio on the side of its cab, that she might avoid the tanker portion of the truck, no doubt full of heating oil since it was headed for the rez, and that she might also push the truck to the side so that it might miss the rear end of the Toyota without sacrificing herself.

It wasn't meant to be, and I watched as I ran with all the muscle I had toward the disaster thirty-six years in the making, but the Charger accelerated in front of the juggernaut and was T-boned into the front entrance of the north tunnel.

An impact of that magnitude carries a concussion all its own, and both Henry and I were having trouble keeping our feet on the slippery, hard surface of the road as the sound came back at us like some gigantic cannon, the screeching sheet metal and twisting sounds of steel against rock like an agonizing shuttle to hell.

Henry was already running as I regained my footing. Miraculously, there was no fire, but the smell of chemicals and mechanical fluids filled the air. The closer you got, the worse it looked; the Dodge was pushed into the mouth of the tunnel as if a bite had been taken out of it with the front of the tanker lodged in there with the hood peeled back over the cab.

Knowing the Cheyenne Nation was a heck of a lot faster than me, I yelled at him, "Get the fire extinguisher from my truck!" Then I pointed toward the tanker. "And get whatever is left of that idiot out of there! I'm going after Rosey!"

He turned and headed back as I tried to find a way into the tunnel past all the debris. Parts were scattered everywhere along with bits of rock and concrete, and although there was antifreeze, transmission fluid, and motor oil on the road, there still wasn't any kind of fuel, and I just hoped the spirit of Bobby Womack or whoever would look down on us with benevolence.

Amazingly, the lights from both vehicles were still operating, one headlight from the tanker shining into the tunnel, where I could see that the Toyopet Crown had been pushed by the impact and was wedged up on the curb about halfway through the tunnel — it looked like neither Sam nor Kimama was moving.

With the cruiser's emergency lights still chasing the length of the tunnel like yellow hounds, I found a space to the left that gave me enough room to edge along beside one of the crumpled orange fenders and get to where I could see the Dodge's black metal. The tanker truck had caught it broadside and pushed it up into the roof, and my only hope was that Rosey had survived in the bubble of the sedan's canopy.

Climbing onto the Rio's crushed bumper, I straddled the metal until I was able to peer into the driver's side of the Charger — Rosey, also motionless, was slumped against the center console.

Luckily, the window was shattered, so I

reached in and, checking her pulse, I was gladdened to feel something. I looked at the configuration of her body's alignment to make sure her neck and spine were intact — it was a gamble to move her, but I was betting it was only a question of time before the whole conglomeration of heating oil, gas, and who knew what was going to come pouring out of the damaged vehicles and we'd be faced with an entirely new catastrophe.

I tried the door, but it didn't budge, the handle coming off in my hand. I growled, slipped the stag-handled knife out of my pocket, flicked it open with my thumb, and, reaching in, sliced through the nylon safety belt. Getting a strong grip on her jacket, I pulled her up through the window and sat her briefly on the sill, where she slumped against me. She was still out cold, with the side of her face scratched up from the implosion of glass and more than a little blood streaming from one nostril — we would be more than lucky if that was the extent of her injuries.

Pulling her over my shoulder, I began the trip down and could see the easiest way would be across the hood of the Dodge rather than the route I had taken to get to her.

I could hear that Henry was spraying the fire extinguisher over the engine area of the Rio. "Is he alive?"

"Yes, is she?"

"Believe it or not, yep — concussed for certain and torn up a bit. I can see Sam and Kimama up ahead, so I'm going to need your help in getting the whole bunch out of here before that tanker decides to rupture and we have a more volatile situation on our hands."

"As soon as I find a way through, I will be there."

I slid off the hood and transferred her from my shoulder to my arms, found solid ground, and stumbled forward, attempting not to lose my precious cargo.

In the combined light of the one headlight from the tanker and the revolving emergency lights on the lopsided Dodge, I carried Rosey to the Toyopet Crown, which was sitting quietly, the motor having of course quit. The front fender of the import was jammed into the rock wall to my right, but other than that it appeared that Sam's keepsake was salvageable.

I gently laid Rosey on the trunk and went around to the driver's-side door, which proved impossible to open, the crumpled front fenders looking to have blocked it.

"Well, hell."

Reaching in the smashed window, I felt the large man's pulse and was satisfied he was simply unconscious. Crossing behind, I took another quick look at Rosey, but she hadn't moved, so I checked on Kimama, also down for the count but still breathing — at least they'd listened and had on their seat belts.

Hearing a noise behind me, I turned to see Henry attempting to get through the tangled mass of twisted metal backlit by the Diamond Rio's Cyclops headlight. "Hurry it up — we have to get this thing away from the wall so we can push it out of here."

I was listening to the Bear's approaching footsteps as I went back around to get a better vantage point in order to push the tiny car when I got a funny feeling and turned back.

Seeing the apprehension on my face, he asked, "Expecting someone else?"

"Never. Where's the fire extinguisher?"

"Out."

"Great." Approaching the driver's side, I reached in past Sam's prodigious belly, shoved the Toyota into neutral, and tried to straighten the steering wheel. I had a little trouble because the fenders were obviously pressing against the inner surface of the tire.

"Why don't we get them out of the car?"

I finally yanked the wheel free enough to straighten the alignment. "Because there are the two of them in there and Rosey on the trunk and Sam weighs over three hundred pounds."

"Good point."

"Push."

He did as I asked, and the mighty Toyopet Crown bounced off the curb and rolled to the middle of the road in a hesitant manner, squealing as the tires rubbed against the wheel wells, grinding it to an uneven halt. "This may prove to be more of a chore than at first thought."

"Yep." Coming around to straighten the wheels again, I joined him, hovering over Rosey, as we began pushing with only minimal results.

"Are you sure it is in neutral?"

"Yep."

"And the emergency brake is off?"

"Yep."

"Is Sam's foot on the brake?"

"That I didn't check." I looked and came back, reporting in. "Negative."

"I do not suppose there is any sense in attempting to start it."

I took a moment to give him my most incredulous look and then continued pushing. We both bore down to the effort when I noticed we were heading in a slight turn toward the other wall. "Keep pushing, and I'll try and straighten the wheel again."

He gave me the look back as he now strained double time.

I reached in and aligned it just as a strange noise came from behind me. I stood up, hearing the clatter of metal on metal, then something sizzling and a long hiss along with the unmistakable sound of liquid hitting the pavement like a cow having a highly combustible piss on a flat rock.

Turning, I stooped and saw a dark reddish liquid filling the gutters on each side of the road and flooding the entire surface as it poured underneath the crashed vehicles and began pooling toward us like arterial blood.

The smell was unmistakable.

"Heating oil."

"Yep." I shifted my gaze to Henry as I rushed to join him at the rear of the Toyota, scrambling to get it and its occupants to the far end of the tunnel and safety.

We pushed as hard as we could, and I could feel the Crown getting easier to move, but we were still making uneven progress. I glanced behind and could see the dyed fluid moving toward us like a tide of red.

■ ■ ■ ■

I don't know where the spark came from, maybe it was something from the engines, or the settling of sheet metal against granite, or more likely the headlight and emergency-light electrics that finally shorted out.

Heating oil needs a catalyst, and I can only guess that there must've been enough gasoline leaking from one of the vehicle tanks to cause it to catch.

The explosion of the vapors was enough to suck both Henry and me from the trunk of the car and away from Rosey, but the flash of heat and disappearance of oxygen was nothing compared to the wall of fire that rose up from the thick oil, now burning blue, that covered the road and continued its relentless crawl toward us.

Deafened by the compression of the explosion in the tunnel, we continued putting our legs into it until the heat of the advancing flames licked at our ankles. Neither Henry nor I was willing to look and see what was happening when another explosion knocked the two of us to our knees.

I hit my head on the chrome bumper and felt the noxious smell of the oil filling my nostrils and throat, causing me to cough and my eyes to water. In the thickening atmosphere, I could hear Henry gagging as well.

I blinked, my eyes burning and my sight blurred, and then blinked again, sure that I could see someone standing in the inferno reflected in the metal, an erect figure with a long slicker and a flat-brimmed hat who seemed to step down from the wreckage and move freely through the walls of flame toward us.

I kept pushing. "You know how he died . . ." Coughing from the clouds of smoke, Kimama's words escaped my lips before I could stop them. With one last look back, I wiped at my eyes, grinding the soot into the wrinkles, but in the wavering heat of the flames couldn't see anything.

Turning my attention forward as the heat became unbearable, all I could think was that if that oil got to us and the gas tank of the Toyopet Crown, we were all going up.

I felt a nudge by my shoulder as someone joined us, pushing both Henry and me to the side, and our speed increased remarkably.

Stealing a glance to my left through the black smoke, I could see him turn his flat-brimmed hat toward me. The lower part of his face was covered by the high collar of his slicker, with only his eyes showing. The eyes stayed on me for a moment, and I had a good look at the darkness in them, almost as if there were no eyes at all until the light caught the slightest glimmer, like the spark that had put us in this precarious situation.

The Crown leaped ahead, and I stumbled to keep up, trying to hold Rosey on the trunk.

After a moment the heat was easier to withstand, and I watched as the front end of the little car crossed through the stark white line of fresh snow as we exited the tunnel. Still pushing the Toyota forward, I glanced to my left again, but the only one there was Henry.

Craning my neck, I looked back, wiping the greasy smut from my eyes. The ghost-like figure was standing at the very edge of the tunnel, backlit by the burning oil, only the brim of his hat and the cuffs on the sleeves of his slicker touched by the moon-light and the falling snow. He looked down as the oil burned, stopping at the snow's edge and sizzling but going no farther. He waited for a moment, looking at me, and then slowly turned and limped back into the hellhole, the flames licking around him and finally swallowing him.

There was another explosion as the second gas tank must've let go, the flames roiling toward us as they burst from the tunnel and rimed the uneven surface of the opening.

Still stumbling backward, I turned and glanced over the quarter panel and could see someone steering the car from outside the driver's-side window.

It was the exact same figure as the one in the tunnel, a figure completely covered by a black slicker that trailed from his covered face to the ankles, where his boots protruded. The same flat-brimmed hat sat on his head as he released the wheel of the tiny car and walked past us back toward the burning tunnel.

In the distance, I could hear approaching sirens from the EMTs, HPs, and Hot Springs County patrols that Henry had no doubt called in while at my truck getting the fire extinguisher.

I glanced over at the Cheyenne Nation just to make sure he was seeing what I was seeing as the figure continued to stand in the middle of the road with its back to us, peering into the conflagration inside.

The Bear returned my glance, and the two of us sat there, propped against the rear bumper of the Toyota, but then his eyes returned to the apparition in front of us.

The specter didn't move for a while, and I half expected him to drop another silver dollar in the middle of the road at the edge of the hissing oil at our feet, but instead he turned, looked at the two of us, and stepped to where we sat on the warm asphalt. He glanced back at the fire and even paused to stoop down to look in the back window at the two unconscious people in the car and the woman lying on the trunk before kneeling and looking first at Henry and then at me. I could plainly see the name tag: WOM-ACK.

His voice was rough but had an almost comical edge as he spoke in the singsong cadence of the Arapaho. "10-78, officer needs assistance."

I stared at him.

He gave one final glance at the whispering edge of the fire that fought a dying cause, and then turned back, popping the metal clasps on the stand-up collar one by one and pulling the black rubber-infused canvas back to reveal his blue eyes — and black, bearded face.

Mike Harlow.

"Boy, you guys sure live dangerously."

EPILOGUE

With the tunnel still blocked, Sam, Kimama, and Rosey were taken south to Riverton, while Coleman, the tanker driver, was brought north to Thermopolis.

Both occupants of the Toyota were concussed, but other than a sprained neck on Kimama and a broken wrist on Sam, they would be fine. The truck driver had a broken leg and nose along with some other complications but would likely be all right, too. Which left us with Rosey, who had whiplash, a dislocated hip, two broken ribs and a broken collarbone, three shattered fingers on her left hand, and a black eye. All in all, I thought she'd gotten off easy.

With blankets layered over top of us, we had waited in the shelter of the middle tunnel as we watched the EMTs load the wounded, all of us drinking strong coffee provided by the Shell station in Shoshoni. Mike Harlow had assisted and then stood a little away, watching the snow collect on the Toyota still sitting in the opening between the tunnels.

"Why?"

It took a second, but the trooper finally turned to look back at Henry and me. "What."

"The radio calls, why?"

He took a deep breath and pulled his slicker apart, and I could see he was dressed in the same sort of clothes I'd seen him in a few days ago. "It was pretty easy. I used a minimal power setup, a scanner with a mic, and hooked it up to a trunking device of my own. I used the tower up there as my transmitter — it's only a half mile from my house. If anybody had tried to triangulate, they would have just come up with that tower at the top of the hill."

"I didn't ask how — I asked why."

He scuffed his boot on the road and walked closer. "I was watching from my place up the canyon and saw the wreck and thought you might need some help."

"That's not the question I asked."

He popped the flat brim of his hat back and shot me a glancing look. "He was my TO, but he was more than that. I'd been back from the military a few years and was working full time at screwing up my life when I put in with the HPs. I was lucky and got Bobby." He shook his head. "One hell of a human being. He helped me straighten myself out and get my shit together in a major way."

I stared back at him but said nothing.

The retired trooper took a step out into the snow, looking up and allowing it to gently strike his face. "He never stole that money, and they treated him like crap over it, never let him live it down. Then, when he died . . ."

"How did he die?"

Harlow laughed and then gestured toward the wreckage in the tunnel. "You just saw an encore performance of it." His arms dropped, and he turned away. "Him and Kimama had this thing going, and she'd come up here to spend a little time with him in the evenings."

"Even when she was babysitting Rosey?"

He turned, nodding his head. "Yeah, he treated that little girl like she was his own, and he'd'a married Kimama except for that asshole husband." He looked back at the crumpled Toyota. "She was driving this crappy Buick station wagon, about as useless as that piece of shit there — stalled out at the same spot, right at the north opening of that tunnel." He paused, collecting his thoughts — or his passions. "Bobby Womack was the bravest and best man I ever met."

"So you wanted to clear his name?"

He turned, savagely this time, a finger pointed at us. "At least keep the legend alive." The hand dropped, and he looked back over his shoulder at the EMTs as they loaded Rosey. "I figured if I made a campaign of it they'd just write me off as some disgruntled retiree. I knew that if Kimama told the story and Rosey remembered, they could clear Bobby. He didn't kill himself, and they were the only ones. He deserved better."

I threw a thumb over my shoulder. "So does she."

He watched as they collapsed the legs on the gurney and pushed Rosey into the van headed for Riverton. "What would you have done? That tanker came around that curve at seventy-five, eighty miles an hour. . . . Everything you love sitting in that conked-out Buick." He turned to look at us again. "What would you have done?" He waited for an answer, but neither of us had one. "I didn't want it to end like this. I never wanted anybody to get hurt, you've got to believe me."

"I do."

He took a deep breath and studied me. "You do?"

I nodded. "I don't approve of your methods, but I'll forgive you for your motive." I sipped my coffee. "That's the problem with actions like this, you never know where they might end — or who might get hurt."

One of the EMTs approached, but then, seeing the seriousness of the conversation, stopped about ten feet away, glancing between Harlow and me. "Sheriff Longmire?"

I answered without looking at him. "Yep?"

"Ms. Wayman says we can't take her until she gets a chance to talk with you."

"Okay, I'll be right there."

Dismissed, he hurried back toward the van. I started after him, Harlow's voice carrying to me in the echo chamber of the tunnel. "You're not turning me in?"

I stopped and tipped my hat back. "I don't see what would be gained by it." I pointed at the Toyopet Crown. "Anyway, you saved us all by helping to push that damn car out of the tunnel."

He was silent for a moment and then did a quick double take at the import. "I doubt I was much help pulling on the door pillar, but at least I got the wheel turned and pointed straight."

I waited a moment before taking a step toward him. "No, I mean before, when you were at the trunk helping push."

He made a face. "What are you talking about?"

I looked at Henry, but he kept his head down and ignored us. "When you came through the tunnel . . ."

He pointed again at the debris-strewn north tunnel, where they were just now using a brace of tow trucks to pull the wreckage from the opening at the far end. "*That* tunnel? Hell no, I came around the path at the other side of the guardrail." He chortled derisively. "No human being could've walked through that."

Unsure of what to say, I turned and moved toward the EMT van as Henry followed, and paused only to ask, "Did you . . . ?"

"What?"

I stared at him as we continued walking. "Did you see . . . ?"

"See what?" He continued to sip his coffee, not making eye contact with me.

I stopped. "The . . ."

"The what?"

I stood there for the briefest of moments and then continued on toward the van and Rosey. "Nothing."

■ ■ ■ ■

"How do I look?"

I leaned in over the gurney. "The black eye is very becoming. Unfortunately, it'll probably be the first thing that heals."

She smiled, and I could see a little blood tracing her gums. "Thank you."

I brushed away the sentiment. "Didn't do anything — at least nothing like you."

"Are they all right?"

"Yep, they're fine. Already on the way to Riverton." I started to straighten. "Where you should be going right now."

I watched as the blanket bulged where she tried to reach out to me with her good hand. "Thank him for me?"

"Who?"

"The trooper."

I laughed. "Harlow? You're lucky if I don't punch his lights out."

"You know who I mean."

I stared at her and then glanced at the Cheyenne Nation, who leaned against the inside of the van, still sipping his coffee.

"We've got to get rolling."

I looked up to see the EMT connecting an IV to Rosey's good arm as two more medics waited at the back doors. "Right,

right . . . We'll get out of the way."

The Bear and I backed out of the van as I gave Rosey's good hand a quick squeeze and then watched as they piled in and closed the doors, switching on the lights and siren and heading south toward Riverton Memorial Hospital.

As we turned and walked back, we saw that they had successfully pried the wreckage from the north tunnel and had dragged it back a good forty feet to where the roadway was now clear. "I guess we can get to my truck now."

Walking through the slushy section between the tunnels, the Bear trailed his hand along a stem of grandfather sage, stripping the leaves from it and holding them up to his nose to smell. "I vote we stay in Thermopolis and head home in the late morning."

"Agreed."

Our footsteps echoed against the black, scorched granite of the tunnel walls as we approached the opening, our boots sticking to the surface of the still-warm asphalt.

The stench was tremendous, so it was good to get to the open air on the other side, making it all that much more puzzling when Henry extended an arm and stopped me just as we stepped out onto the thin layer of snow, stained red, green, and black from the leaking wreckage.

I looked down at the back of his fist against my chest and then at him.

He thumped the fist against me again, holding it out as if it held something. "Toss this into the tunnel and then say your piece."

I opened a hand under his, and he dumped the sage leaves into it.

"Always have incense." He started off toward my truck, turned slightly as he went, and looked back at me. "You can tell Heeci'ecihit you understand him, if you think it means anything to him."

I stood there for a moment watching him go and then thought about just tossing the leaves and following, but then I remembered Kimama's warning that I needed to respect the beliefs of people who had been in this part of the world thousands of years before mine.

Turning back, I planted both feet and made ready to speak when I noticed the same great horned owl sitting on the rocks above the opening of the tunnel. "Well, hello, you. I would've thought that all that sound and fury would've driven you off." His large head turned, and the great golden eyes looked down at me. "I don't suppose you'd like to deliver a message, would you?"

He only blinked once and continued to watch me.

"I guess I'll have to do it myself." Gazing into the tunnel, I cleared my throat and called out, "Heeci' . . . Heeci'ecihit." Giving up on the Native pronunciation, I dropped it and just spoke. "Bobby, if you're in there, and I don't think you are, then, um . . . thanks." I took another step forward and looked around in the scorched darkness. "You did good. You always did good, but it's over now and you can move along." I tossed the sage leaves in, a few of them sticking to my hand, and stood there looking into the darkness. "And here I am, talking to an empty tunnel."

Shrugging, I turned and started to walk away as a single 1888-O Hot Lips Morgan silver dollar fell out of the darkness; it bounced and rolled toward me, stopping on the thin layer of new snow and then falling over faceup just as the great horned owl unfurled his prodigious wings and batted them twice before sailing over my head and gliding up the canyon out of sight.

Now, a lot of people might believe that it was something else that caused what happened next, but I'm firmly of the belief that the concussion from the impact of the two vehicles and the subsequent explosions must've loosened their resting place, as close to a thousand of the same coins cascaded from the ceiling of the tunnel like a jackpot, bouncing and rolling in every direction.

At least that's our story, the owl and me.

ABOUT THE AUTHOR

Craig Johnson is the author of thirteen previous novels in the Walt Longmire series. The Walt Longmire series is the basis for the hit A&E drama, *Longmire.* Johnson has a background in law enforcement and education. He lives in Ucross, Wyoming, population twenty-five.